COMMITTEE OF DETAIL

A CONSTITUTIONAL GHOST STORY

BY

SAM WALKER

Silent Record Publications
PO Box 623
Bayside, California 95524

PART I

President-elect Adriana Hernandez grew up in Tucson, Arizona. Her father had come to Arizona from Mexico as a child and her mother immigrated just before the two were married. A diesel truck mechanic, Mr. Hernandez learned much of his trade during his four years in the United States Army. After the last of her five children went to school Mrs. Hernandez began working in a supermarket, starting as a checker and becoming assistant manager after five years.

Religion was very important to both parents. Raised as Catholics, they brought their children to mass at least once a week and always prayed before meals. They did not accept every church policy and were not afraid of some debate among their friends and fellow parishioners. But they maintained exceptional moral standards and enforced them rigidly with their children.

They also insisted that Hernandez and her four younger siblings learn both English and Spanish, even designating certain parts of the week as English- or Spanish-only. This was difficult for Mrs. Hernandez, since she did not even begin to learn English until she arrived in Tucson; however, she never let the frustration show and never pleaded for exceptions. As a result, Hernandez became fluent in both languages.

Pondering the legal profession as a possible career, during her final year of high school Hernandez worked as a file clerk and part-time receptionist for a small law office, a job she continued after entering the University of Arizona. The firm primarily handled personal injury cases and she helped with intake and subsequent communications with Spanish-speaking clients. She enjoyed the work she did, but the attorneys she worked for did not inspire any enthusiasm for practicing law, especially personal injury.

Following her second year at U of A, and needing some new experience away from her family, she joined the Air Force. She served four years, finishing as an Airman First Class. For much of her tour she worked as a Technical Operations Specialist assigned to the 55th Rescue Squadron, performing search and rescue missions.

Deployed to the Mediterranean on the eve of Operation Desert Storm, she spent hundreds of hours standing by for missions into hostile territory aboard the HH-60 recovery helicopter assigned to her unit. The chopper came under enemy fire several times, but was not hit. She later described the experience as very frightening; nevertheless, the disciplined calm she felt as shells exploded near by increased substantially her confidence for dealing with difficult circumstances.

Service in the Air Force also enhanced her social confidence. With so much time in the close company of other men and women, she overcame an innate shyness, became assertive, and developed a natural charisma that drew many strangers into her circle.

Following her discharge Hernandez returned to Tucson and resumed her undergraduate studies at Arizona, tuition paid by the US government, no housing or other costs of living because she lived at home with her parents and younger sister. Majoring in economics, she planned for graduate school, but was convinced by her family to choose law school instead.

A number of schools accepted her. She picked UCLA: Out of state while only a nine-hour drive from home. Hernandez did well the first year, although not well enough to make law review. Not eager to master the academic aspects of law, her grade record declined increasingly through the second and third year, in part because she devoted so much time to volunteer work with the El Centro legal clinics.

Through these clinics UCLA law students provided legal

services to a variety of communities in the greater Los Angeles area.   From her first day at the Youth Deportation Clinic Hernandez' commitment to the work there, and at many of the other 15 El Centro clinics, steadily increased. She became a clinic chair, then a training director for the entire program.

After graduating with a JD degree, Hernandez moved back to Tucson and began her career as a prosecutor in the district attorney's office. She made this decision because, despite her constant longing for space between her and her family, they were more important to her well-being than she consciously admitted.

Except for her brother Tony, who enlisted in the United States Army and was posted for an extended time in the Philippines, Hernandez' family remained in the Tucson area. Her other brother, Eric, became a pharmacist, manager of a supermarket pharmacy, husband, and father of three, two girls and a boy. Her sister Pamela obtained a certificate in Hotel Management from Pima Community College and worked for several hotel chains before marrying one of the executives and staying at home with five children. Ten years younger than Adrianna, Jennifer Hernandez was starting her first year at U of A when Adrianna moved back to Tucson for good.

After a week at the office, the DA assigned Hernandez to the prosecution of gang-related crimes. She brought her first case against two 19-year-old members of the Clan de Acero, charged with armed robbery of a Denny's restaurant at 2:30 in the morning. Guilty. But she did not feel like celebrating.

Nor did she ever assume the competitive desire to "win", to build a record of successful prosecutions, that characterized many prosecutors. For Hernandez it was a job to get done. And as long as she did what was needed to obtain a conviction, she felt that she had gotten the job done, whatever the result. Plus she could never wall off her sensitivity to the human aspect of every case. With each conviction she saw another person's life wasted.

At the beginning of her second year, she prosecuted a case that attracted unusual publicity. It also involved the Clan de Acero. They were charged with several offenses arising from their efforts to recruit male high school students for the gang and underaged girls for prostitution. Their "pitch" included offerings of drugs and alcohol, threats of harm to victims and family, and protection. To demonstrate the seriousness of their threats they kidnapped the six-year-old son of an undocumented Mexican family and put photographs online of him hanging upside down from the rafters in a garage.

From the day the DA assigned her the case Hernandez almost daily received anonymous warnings that her safety was in danger. Aside from adding to the anxiety expected for a case like that, and the unrelenting tension resulting from the urgent need to convict and incarcerate these monsters, the warnings did not affect her handling of the prosecution.

Less disturbing, but more annoying, were the frequent intrusions by local, and sometimes national, reporters trying to discover her evidence and the identify of her witnesses. She was asked many times to comment on the difficult legal issues presented by the DA's decision to arrest and prosecute the gang as a whole. Did she really expect the court to buy her theories of conspiracy and criminal racketeering? Declining to speak about anything specific to the case, Hernandez nevertheless defended the merit of the law she would ask to be applied and she did it in plain language that would be understood by the community at large, not just lawyers.

In the end, the judge accepted her theories for the most part and the jury found enough evidence to convict on a majority of the counts. The strikingly stiff sentences got the attention of all Tucson gang members. And Adrianna Hernandez became a city hero.

Not in her own mind however. Again she had done only

what she was paid to do. And putting young men in jail was not really going to solve the problems of society.

More rewarding for her were the volunteer hours she spent working to counteract the influence of gangs on teenagers, Hispanic teenagers in particular. Under the auspices of a community group that provided unofficial and informal counseling in high schools for boys who had been approached about joining a gang, she spent the few hours she could spare each week talking to anxious boys. She did the same through a program run by the Catholic Diocese of Tucson.

As a result of her work as a deputy DA and in the community, Hernandez developed an extensive network of acquaintances who shared similar concerns for the well-being of the city. Two years into her tenure with the DA's office many of these people urged her to run for a spot on the city council. Once she mentioned this casually to her family her reluctance was overwhelmed by their relentless insistence that she do it.

From the day she filed an army of relatives and friends trekked through Ward 3 knocking on doors and talking to anyone who would listen. Jennifer designed an exquisite flyer that they plastered everywhere they could find a spot. Because Hernandez already was well-known throughout the city, she benefitted from local news coverage that ignored other candidates. She also was one of the first local candidates to exploit the nascent power of social media.

Elected to serve a four-year term, and since the members of the council were paid only as part-time officials, Hernandez at first intended to remain with the DA's office. Some question arose, however, about whether a new city code provision prohibiting council members from holding other civil positions applied to criminal prosecutors. Rather than test the issue, she resigned from the DA's office, a decision she did not regret in the slightest, having grown weary of putting people in jail.

With no real income, she continued to live with her parents and devoted her time to the kind of legal aide projects she had enjoyed so much at UCLA. Because she had free time the other councilmembers did not, because she enjoyed it immensely, and because she had become extraordinarily good at it, she also volunteered to fill every request that came in for a member of the council to attend a function and speak.

She even occasionally spoke at events promoting policies she was opposed to, surprising and angering the organizers, and ensuring that she would not receive any future invitations. Nearly all such events concerned some proposal that would have required an increase in spending, supported by a sales tax hike, a new bond issue, or raising a fee.

Aligned with so-called "liberal" views on many issues, Hernandez was solidly conservative with respect to fiscal matters. Combined with her somewhat fanciful belief that she could persuade anyone to at least reconsider a position, this faith in public thrift cast her into a few awkward, sometimes tense and hostile, appearances. A remarkable aspect of her conduct in these circumstances, however, was that in the end she made friends, not enemies, and earned respect for being so forthright and courageous, for being able to denounce an opinion while uplifting the persons who held it.

One evening, just under a year after the election, Hernandez attended a symposium on immigration and language education at the University of Arizona. She was not a scheduled speaker, but rose to comment and was then identified as a member of the city council. Afterwards, she was approached by a man of about 32 years, with dark bushy hair, and a full mustache.

An assistant professor of linguistics, he expressed interest in her statements about youth crime and education, introduced himself as Owen Beck, and after they talked for a few minutes, asked if he could buy her a drink or a cup of coffee. She accepted the offer. They sat in an off campus coffeeshop talking for two hours and then commenced a relationship. Strictly platonic at first, within a month they became intimate, and six months later decided to marry.

Their preference for a small private ceremony could not withstand the family pressure for a full-blown Catholic wedding complete with a full mass and a festa with more than 300 guests, cases of champagne, and food provided by the finest Mexican caterer in Tucson. The event was featured on local news programs and photographs showed up on numerous websites.

Adrianna and Owen then flew to New York City for a 5-day honeymoon. Two Broadway shows, a Yankees game, the Metropolitan Museum of Art, eight elegant restaurants, and hours of passion alone in their hotel room. Although she had experienced sex a couple of times before, it had been nothing whatsoever like it was with Owen and the added effect of the truest love.

Adrianna longed to have a child. So did Owen, but he was more patient and better able to see down the road. As the honeymoon came to a close they discussed it frequently. The morning of their departure back to the real world Owen told Adrianna he thought they should wait. Wait for what? she responded. Wait until you are elected mayor. He then went into an extended harangue insisting that she must run and disclosing that he already had mentioned it to her family, with the expected result.

Stunned, flattered, and uncertain, Adrianna promised to think about it. But there was a crowd of family and friends waiting for them at the airport in Tucson, many holding up signs that read "Adrianna for Mayor" and more chanting "Mayor Adrianna". Adrianna Hernandez hated to disappoint people.

So it was that the campaign began. Shortly after the

incumbent mayor announced that he would not seek another term and that he strongly supported Hernandez to succeed him. Once again Adrianna's Army fanned out -- this time across the city – joined by more than 200 new volunteers. With unusually weak competition, Hernandez won by a substantial margin and became Mayor of Tucson, Arizona.

Because the mayor had only slightly more powers and responsibilities than members of the council, however, the new job was pretty much the same in terms of what she was required to do. More ceremonies, more promotion of the city, more recognition, more dignitary status. Indeed, Hernandez attracted national attention when Newsweek included her in a piece about young mayors in border regions who were trying novel approaches to handling influxes of undocumented immigrants. The article pointed out, however, that she was decidedly opposed to spending more public money on the problem. She was, the author noted, "very fiscally conservative".

But with no significant new demands on her time, she continued the charged pace of her volunteer work, routinely putting in 80-hour weeks, though often working from the home she and Owen rented. Their time together was limited, but joyful for the most part, and exciting for them if only for how precious it was. It also turned out to be productive. Fifteen months after the election Hernandez became pregnant.

She did not slow down her hectic schedule. More and more photos of her appeared online as her belly expanded and by the eighth month she was a national celebrity of sorts. There were not many pregnant mothers serving as mayors of large cities.

And she often would appear in photos taken in somewhat incongruous locations: on street corners in tough neighborhoods talking to a group of tough-looking young men, riding a bicycle for the start of a city-sponsored bike race, filling out a formal suit tailored for maternity wear as she rode standing on a Sun Link streetcar declining offers to take someone's seat or stood at a podium speaking and distributing civic awards.

Twins. A boy and a girl. Luis and Sara.

Now Hernandez saw that she needed to cool off her dynamo and reserve time for her children. She began to regret becoming mayor. She wanted to resign. She wanted to stay at home for as long as she felt Luis and Sara needed her.

Once again, however, her family's influence swayed her. Owen and Jennifer were especially vehement. There was no need for such sacrifice, they said. As a college professor Owen had abundant flexible time that he could spend at home. And Jennifer was most eager to be Adrianna's surrogate for any childcare duties necessary. So while she did reduce a bit the number of hours she put in every week, she did not do so to the extent anyone would notice. And rather than resigning, she attracted an even brighter spotlight.

Unopposed for reelection, Hernandez began her second term amidst early speculation that she might run for governor of Arizona in the next election, which would occur in three years. Several prominent political, business, and community leaders urged her to consider it.

She said no. And kept saying no whenever asked. Instead she began to happily anticipate the day she could cast off all the responsibilities of public office and become the stay-at-home mom she believed her children needed. So the gubernatorial election passed, re-installing the incumbent.

Hernandez served out the remaining year of her tenure and left politics for a domestic life: helping Luis and Sara with their homework, dropping them off at school, picking them up later for some fun activity she never had time for before. To those who cautioned her to be wary of paralyzing boredom she said not to worry – she was going to write a book.

The book was to be a response to what she perceived as an

increasing attack on family, cultural, and moral traditions. This attack was the root of disorder in society, she would argue. She had experienced it firsthand as a prosecutor and municipal leader. The most salient symptom she would identify as the new predominance of gang codes over traditional rules of behavior and living among young men and women.

For two years she devoted her time to Owen, Luis, and Sara, cared for her parents when they needed it, cooked molotes, tamales, and albóndigas for family festas, learned from Owen's aunt how to make cottage pie and farl, grew zinnias, daylilies, snapdragons, cilantro, and basil in a garden along the side of the backyard, helped organize fundraisers for the school, did laundry, cleaned the house, and gossiped with other homemaker moms on her block. She did not finish the book.

However, she did write many components of it, and these were published separately in various journals. Hernandez also nurtured her network of contacts within the political, business, legal, and law enforcement communities. She accepted numerous invitations to speak at public and private functions throughout the state. After the two years she was more widely known in Arizona than she had been as mayor of Tucson.

She also was bored as heck and ready to resume a career in politics. Pleas for her to run for governor again came from diverse sources, including some with money available to support the campaign of a well-known fiscal conservative. This time she said yes.

Competing against three other candidates for the primary election, Hernandez touted her tough budgeting practices as mayor, her aggressive campaigns to reduce crime, and her unprecedented experiments with programs to help the poor. The growing Hernandez extended family, including cousins, in-laws, aunts, and uncles dedicated their free time to the campaign. As did hundreds of people who had become acquainted with

Hernandez over the years.

Hernandez herself visited every county. She traveled in a custom bus outfitted with a small platform that could be erected outside the rear door, "ADRIANNA por ARIZONA" displayed across the sides of the bus in giant red, white, and blue letters. Regardless of the demographics of each community, she always gave part of her speech in Spanish.

The primary was close, but Hernandez won. Her opponent in the general election was a veteran United States Representative who had held his seat for 18 years. He hammered her lack of experience, focusing especially on her time out of politics, even referring to her a few times as a "soccer mom" who did not have the broad perspective needed to be an effective governor. The "professionals" advising Hernandez told her to fight back by painting her opponent as an over the hill hack out of touch with today's critical issues. She chose engaging magnanimity instead.

The congressman, she responded, as an elder statesman, possessed wisdom she did not yet have. The voters should seriously consider his views. On the other hand, she said, it was not certain that 18 years as a representative in Washington brought a broader perspective than did four years in the Air Force, two terms as mayor of Arizona's second largest city, and a few years hands on experience in raising a family.

The congressman came out of the primary with a double-digit lead in the polls. This only further energized the organization that had produced a primary victory for Hernandez. She accelerated the already frenetic pace of her campaign, routinely speaking six or more times a day, soldiering through hour after hour shaking hands and conversing in two languages.

The final polls showed the race virtually tied. However, when all precincts had reported Hernandez led, although by less than 3,000 votes. A recount seemed inevitable. Yet her opponent, exhausted and ill, demurred and conceded. Hernandez became governor of Arizona.

2

The state being one of the few without a governor's mansion, she at first continued to live in the house she and Owen rented. But it soon became evident that a much larger and nicer residence was needed. Hernandez was not one to relish the trappings of power and position; however, she believed it was important to maintain some mark of her status. Plus there would be expectations of social activities, dinners, cocktail parties, etc., which required more house than they had.

So when one of her wealthier supporters offered to lease them a grand Victorian three-story six-bedroom house with a palatial office and elegant formal dining room for no more rent than they currently paid, they accepted. Adrianna, Owen, Luis, and Sara moved in. So did Jennifer. So did Adrianna's parents.

Her personality always a potent combination of aggressiveness and charm, Governor Hernandez determined to establish a personal relationship with every member of the legislature. There is no reason or justification, she believed, for a political leader to have enemies.

Consequently, during her first term she was determined to veto legislation in only the most extreme circumstances. Only when her extraordinary powers of persuasion and negotiation failed to produce an acceptable compromise on a bill that would require new revenue and spending did she even consider a veto. She routinely disregarded party lines in consulting on issues and directing policy initiatives. Her judicial and executive branch appointments also reflected unprecedented diversity, in terms of party, sex, race, ethnicity, and sexual preference.

It was critical for her that the people of Arizona, from heads of the opposition party to undocumented workers surviving on menial labor, understand that whatever her policies she followed them with sincerity. To Hernandez honesty was not a disingenuously projected image.   It was a fundamental component of her being.

Because of this, and despite her wish to avoid animosity, she did profess some controversial beliefs. Almost obsessed with the importance of family in combatting crime, she proposed revisions to the Criminal and Marital and Domestic Relations codes that would have mandated certain conduct by parents concerning their children. Her idea was to make it a criminal offense for a parent, for example, to skip a parent-teacher conference or fail to attend activities in which the child participated. However, the difficulty of enforcement persuaded Hernandez to drop the proposal before a formal bill was drafted. But not before it received widespread attention in the national media.

As did her successful programs to reduce spending by the state government, to restructure state support of public education to reward efficiency and technological improvements, to establish more court-annexed resources for helping juveniles to use criminal charges as opportunities for life changes, and to create mandatory Spanish language instruction for public safety employees.

She won re-election by the largest majority in Arizona history.

In her second term she courted more controversy. Consistent with her catholic religious beliefs, she regarded abortion as a sinful and selfish act, but she also believed that the government had no power or right to interfere with a woman's choice of what happens in her body. This did not mean for her, however, that the government could or should promote or sponsor abortions in any manner. So while she steadfastly opposed any legislation that would criminalize abortion, or punish women or doctors for it, she also opposed any laws that would cause the state government to spend public money to pay for or subsidize the procedure.

Fortunately, although provoking heated debate, Hernandez' views were not put to the ultimate test of a veto. The two bills that would have subsidized abortions for certain groups of low-income women were amended before final passage to eliminate that consequence. The governor's role in securing the amendment was never disclosed and her public popularity was not affected.

During the final two years of her tenure Hernandez concentrated her remarkable energy and charisma on bringing more industry and investment to the state. For this she traveled extensively, logging more days outside the state than any previous governor.

Three factors made this possible: 1. She enjoyed flying, a residual benefit of her Air Force experience. 2. She had grown comfortable going about the world alone – traveling, socializing, attending meetings solo, with no escort, partner, sidekick, pal, assistant, or husband. 3. Jennifer ... or Aunt Jenny, as Luis and Sara called their second mom.

The governor's efforts succeeded in attracting some new investment, although not to the extent she had hoped for. To her pitch pointing to the restraints on taxes she had managed to impose over the years prospective investors responded: Yes, but the state's term limits will ensure that you are no longer governor by the time our projects come to fruition. They were highly skeptical of her assurance that the new governor would continue the fiscal frugality. Even if she or he intended to, the investors said, no new governor could equal her personal power for effecting that agenda.

While Hernandez did not bring a mass of investments to Arizona, however, she did greatly expand her circle of acquaintances. Very few people who met her did not want to meet her again. Visits to other states invariably led to invitations to return. So by the time she left office the name Adrianna Hernandez was more than familiar to business and political people throughout the most populous states.

She also had become somewhat of a legend and a household word among the general public. Largely because of one incident. It happened in Chicago, at the Spanish Consulate, where Hernandez had arranged to meet with two wealthy Spanish venture capitalists.   As the meeting was about to conclude a loud commotion arose outside the conference room, in the lobby of the consulate. An official burst into the room and stammered that armed men had entered the office, pointing weapons at everyone, threatening to shoot if not obeyed.

The three men in the room were terrified. They looked at each other with wild eyes and trembled. One of them pulled out a cell phone, but he could not keep his hands steady enough to use it.

Hernandez, however, although tense, settled into an icy calm. Contacting police with her cell phone, she was told that they knew all about it already, that the intruders were Catalonian separatist radicals, and that they were demanding $100 million, transportation to the airport for themselves and an unknown number of the consulate employees to be taken as hostages. If the demand was not satisfied within one hour, they would begin to execute the people now trapped in the office.

Hernandez then rose and went to the door. The men stared at her in disbelief as she opened the door and went out. Shouting in Spanish and sobbing echoed through the corridor. Approaching the lobby entrance, she was suddenly confronted by the barrel of a high-powered rifle.

"On the knees now!" a male voice with a heavy accent shouted very close to her side.

"Soy la gobernadora de Arizona," she said looking straight ahead. "Yo valgo más para ti que estas personas. Déjalos ir y lléveme a mi". One of the bilingual clerks on the floor whispered a translation to another: "I am the governor of Arizona. I am worth more to you than these people. Let them go and take me".

Consternation and confusion gripped the four men holding weapons. They studied Adrianna like she was some kind of alien being and mumbled to each other something she could not hear.

"We take you with them," one called from across the lobby.

"That would be stupid," Hernandez answered, her throat tight and her back sweating. "How far can you get with a crowd?"

"Shut up!" Two, who appeared to be leading the "mission", conferred again. Then one motioned for the guy jabbing his gun into her side to bring her to a chair behind a counter. There they tied her hands behind her back and wheeled her into a closet.

As the time passed heart-poundingly slowly, the only sounds that penetrated the closet door into the dark within were incoherent shouting and occasional bumps against walls. Eventually – she had no idea how long – there was a few quick loud pops she guessed to be gunfire, followed soon after by someone calling her name in clear English. She pushed the chair into the door to make an alerting sound. The door was opened by an officer in SWAT gear.

Two of the bad guys were dead, two on their way to the hospital. It turned out that the men Hernandez had met with, after hearing her exchange with the Catalonians, had mastered their nerves enough to let the police know what was happening. The negotiator then convinced the gang that, since they held the governor hostage holding the others was not necessary for their objective, and that no attempt would be made to satisfy their demands unless and until they released everyone but her. After some very agitated discussion, they complied, let everyone else go, and were just about to retrieve her from the closet to serve as a shield when the SWAT force entered and opened fire.

For twenty-four hours no story topped it across the news media universe. In a matter of hours the governor of Arizona became a huge sensation throughout the connected world. Her office was bombarded with requests for interviews, her staff telling all that the requests would be forwarded to her in Chicago.

It was not until she closed and bolted her hotel room door and saw herself in a wall mirror that she felt the shock. The crying erupted like a convulsion. Shuddering uncontrollably as she realized what she had done and how very close she had been to very real harm.

Unable to speak with anyone, she already had turned off her phone. Her family would know she was all right. She was sorely tempted by the bottles of wine, vodka, and scotch available to her in the minibar. But did not give in. Instead she filled the tub with the hottest water, undressed, sank into it, and soaked there for more than an hour.

It helped. More calm, though still anxious, she turned on the phone. The voicemail was full with nineteen messages. The texts exceeded capacity. Rather than listening to and reading everything she called the office in Tucson and learned of the interview requests.

No interviews, she told the staff. She would not talk about the incident to anyone except her family. No exceptions. Do not even bother to ask no matter who makes the request.

When she felt enough in control to keep from crying, she

called Owen. At first, he was frantic and angry, about what she did, but more because he had not been able to reach her. Then he melted and thanked God she was okay. She talked to Luis and Sara and Jennifer and by the end was bawling like a baby.

3

Hernandez finished her term thankful for term limits. Her energy and taste for public life had dissipated. After an emotional farewell, she retreated once more into domestic serenity. Except that she was anything but serene. Her dynamo began to power up within a few weeks and she grew restless and irritable, a development complained about repeatedly by Owen, then Jennifer, then Luis and Sara, now in their early teens and decidedly unafraid to speak bluntly.

So protracted discussions, and occasional bitter arguments, eventually produced a family consensus: Adrianna must get back into it. So she accepted some of the numerous invitations she had received to appear on television. She was frequently contacted for comments for evening and morning news segments, appeared on English and Spanish language talk shows, and even once guest starred as herself on a Spanish language novela. Afterwards she considered this a mistake, regarding the experience as "fun" but trivial.

Much more meaningful for her were the written commentaries, essays, and guest columns she contributed to a variety of national publications. Her topics ranged from the need for a compassionate immigration policy coupled with strengthened border security to proposals for drastic reductions of the government bureaucracy to encouraging participation by more women in law enforcement and municipal government.

With the family's unanimous and hearty approval, she

embarked on another trip. The next presidential election was eighteen months off. She wanted to be part of it, to endorse, then consult and campaign for, someone. So the agenda for her trip included meetings with advisers for the crowded field of candidates, and with the candidates themselves. Her name and fame opened any door she tried. They also required her to decline repeated suggestions that she declare herself a candidate for president or that she at least challenge the incumbent Arizona senator.

By January of the election year there were two frontrunners for her party's nomination – Mike Jordan, the senior senator from Ohio, and Wallace Borger, former governor of Minnesota and current president of Columbia University. Jordan, the younger of the two by 25 years, with swarthy ruggedness that dominated the television screen, was an electric speaker and an extraordinarily charismatic campaigner. His problem, Hernandez believed, was a somewhat wishy-washy attitude towards real issues – maybe exactly what the country needs, her brothers joked.

Borger's chief drawback was his age: 75. And he looked it, although boasting that he was in excellent health. Determined to brush off the issue, which, of course, no one talked about openly, Borger tried repeatedly to demonstrate his fitness. He ran five miles every day and made sure press cameras followed him. He challenged his colleagues to tennis matches and would display his sagging but slender physique with swimming and diving sessions. During a couple of joint appearances with Jordan Borger told him they should play one on one basketball to decide the nomination.

And he was anything but wishy washy. As with many older people, he had formed definite opinions on almost every matter and stated them with hard conviction. Some Hernandez agreed with, some she did not. Nevertheless, she respected

Borger enormously and was prepared to endorse and work for him if he demonstrated enough strength in the early contests.

The Iowa caucuses were inconclusive. But Jordan and his supporters did a much better job of spinning a victory. So he had a slight edge in momentum going into New Hampshire.

It seemed that Borger's style was not resonating well with younger voters. While he could be very avuncular when needed, his overall image was of a staid and stiff elder who probably would have preferred to campaign the way presidents did in the 19th Century – from the front porch of his home, the media coming to him, instead of he having to go out among the masses shaking hands interminably and eating corn dogs that upset his stomach.

The New Hampshire polls, and those in the states whose primaries would follow, began to show Borger's chances slipping away. And the more he campaigned the bleaker the outlook became. Accordingly, Hernandez was compelled to conclude that her support for Borger likely would be wasted and that she thus would miss an opportunity to work for the winning side.

However, her sentiment was with Borger and she felt great affection for him personally. So, having decided to endorse Jordan, she wanted to communicate her decision directly to Borger in hopes that she could soften its effect.

She waited until the New Hampshire results confirmed the expected, then telephoned an acquaintance who was close to Borger.

"Hi Silvia, Adrianna Hernandez."

"Adrianna! What a nice surprise. How are things in the desert?"

"We actually had a little rain yesterday. "

"Guess you know about New Hampshire. Stupid granite staters. Don't know a gem from a horse's ass."

"Yeah, that's a shame. I really thought he had a chance."

"Not against Jingle Jangle Jordan."

"Best not repeat that to me. See I called to see if I can talk with him, to tell him how much I revere him, but—"

"But you're joining the Jordan show."

"Well your guy's not going to continue, is he? Looks like it's over. Why --"

"I'm sorry Adrianna. I know you need to do it. I don't think he has decided his next move. I know he thinks very highly of you and was looking forward to campaigning with you, if you came on board. I will let him know you called and want to talk with him. Please don't do anything until you hear back from me or someone else here. Ok?"

"Of course."

Two hours later Sylvia called back. "He wants to talk to you, but not on the phone. He's in New York. Any chance you can go there?"

No chance, Hernandez said to herself. But to Sylvia: "I don't know. I don't understand why he won't do it by phone. I just wanted to extend a courtesy."

"I know what he will say. He'll say it's too important to do over the phone. He did say to tell you he is pretty sure you will not regret it."

Annoyed, mildly excited, thinking over the details, searching for a way to excuse herself and finding none appropriate, flipping through the calendar to see when the science fair would be, mentally noting to discuss with husband and kids before committing, she said "Let me see what I can do. How soon do you need to know?"

"Half hour enough?" Silvia said chuckling. "Obviously sooner the better, but you just let me know when you know. And another thing: Best to keep a lid on it. Tell whoever you have to, but that's it."

There really was no decision to make. She could not disappoint the old man. Bailing on his campaign would be bad enough; refusing to tell him in person when invited to do so would make it much worse. Accustomed as they were to her physical absences, and very proud of everything she did, her family firmly insisted that she go.

So she went. The next day, landing at LaGuardia at 2:30 in the afternoon. Taxi through strangely light traffic. In Borger's reception area at Columbia, where she was greeted by a dampened-looking young man with a loosened tie hanging from his neck.

"Ms. Hernandez. I'm Rich Gardner, one of Mr. Borger's assistants. I hope your trip went well. He is waiting for you." Gardner motioned for her to proceed into the sumptuous office.

"Adrianna!" Borger greeted her with a genuine smile and arms open for a hug. "I am so glad you came. So glad." He pointed to the two other people who had jumped up respectfully. "Perhaps you know Brooke Spencer and Reggie Wright, heads of my campaign staff." Then he waved in the direction of a tall, blond, 20-something and athletic man hovering towards the corner. "And my grandson, Karl."

Gardner disappeared and the discussion began among the politicians and staff sitting on facing sofas. Karl continued to hover.

"I hope we can go straight to the heart of the matter," Borger said. "I know you have come to tell me you are planning to endorse Jordan, so now you don't have to tell me. But I have something to tell you, Adrianna. To offer you actually. You see I may be old and senile, but I'm not completely out of touch. I know at least one of the big reasons we're not succeeding is my campaign style. I am no match for the Jordan Juggernaut. I expect too much. I expect people to listen to what I have to say. But it doesn't work that way any more. And I am damn sure not going to reboot my personality.

"So let me just get it out there. Adrianna, you are a

remarkable person, an extraordinary political actor. You're not just contemporary; you are way ahead. People, all kinds of people, are attracted to you. They listen to you. More importantly, you make sure they do. You have all the tools I don't. So here's my proposal. I want you to join my campaign. Full-time. With me and without me. Wherever and whenever needed. In consideration for this commitment I promise, if we get the nomination, to select you to join the ticket as candidate for Vice President of the United States."

Hernandez was stunned. She sat silent, starring at Borger as if he had lost his mind, accounting for all the trivial realities in the room to convince herself that Borger's words were real as well. And when the idea finally crystalized in her mind her first reaction was an overpowering no.

An incredible honor, she told Borger. Did not deserve it. So many others more qualified. Would be a big mistake. No national experience. No international expertise. Never campaigned outside Arizona. Not ready. Family not ready. Country not ready.

It came out as a burst of soft-spoken babbling, almost a plea for him to take it back, to rewind himself and proceed again with a different finish. But that was not going to happen. Borger listened to her patiently. This response was obviously what he expected.

When she paused, he told her how he understood, that he did not want her to decide anything right then, just not to categorically rule it out, to go back home and tell the family what a crazy old man he is and what a ridiculous idea he has. Until informed otherwise, he will assume that she does not want it and proceed with his deliberations about the future.

Spencer and Wright both chimed in almost simultaneously cautioning her about telling anyone but family about the discussion.

Borger knew his mark.   Hernandez' family was unanimously incredulous that she would even have to think twice about accepting. "Opportunidad milagroso!" "Serás una Latina de fama mundial!" What if we lose? "He may lose. You can only win … the hearts of the people." What if I make a mistake, a major gaffe? "Don't pretend to be afraid. You are the most courageous Latina I ever knew. The People will love and follow you. Sin duda!"

The identity of Borger's running mate if he should win the nomination was the worst kept secret in many an election year. That is exactly how he wanted it.   No formal decision or announcement. Always the same answer to reporters' insistent questioning: "I would be honored to have her on the ticket. But no decision has been made.   All of us must wait for the convention."

Meanwhile Hernandez' adventure began with intensive study of international issues.   Within hours after she communicated her acceptance of Borger's offer multiple memoranda arrived from his advisers. They covered such a wide range of topics that the depth of each was minimal. Still she was able to soak up key facts about the fluid policy on trade with China, controversial arms sales to Saudi Arabia, status of talks, accords, and potential treaties involving Israel, the Palestinians, and other fertile crescent countries, dilemmas complicating oil and gas transportation between Russia and the European Union, possible fallout from destabilization in Iran, reciprocal trade agreements with South American countries, US' capacity for supporting security and democracy among the countries of Africa, and so on.

Most of what she read she already was familiar with. The purpose of the self-study, however, was to learn the Borger perspective on the issues and, almost as important, to master the language and analytical methods commonly used in discussing international matters. Whatever her lack of expertise, Borger's people explained, Hernandez must at least sound like she knows the issues. As a somewhat seasoned and pragmatic female politician, she was prepared for patronizing and able to ignore its insulting aspects.

More irksome to her was the well-intended schooling on appearance. Already known for her modest and traditional yet elegant formal wardrobe, she bristled at the "guidance" conveyed on the subject by Borger's public relations consultants. She must eschew hairstyles that were too short, they said, because she might come off as a closet lesbian. Don't feed me this bullshit, she fired back. That ended the lessons.

Hernandez was well aware of the power her visual presence could exert on the attitude of many voters. She was hardly naïve enough to believe that women in politics would not be judged, at least subconsciously, by the hairstyles they chose, the clothes they wore, their make-up or lack thereof. She also knew the power of images on television and computer screens. Determined to always exhibit an attractive mien, while radiating intelligence, capability, and courage, Hernandez did not need coaching.

She normally wore her nails short, small but classy earrings, her dark brown hair neatly fixed at shoulder length, and colorful, put-together clothing ensembles. This style would not change just to suit some professional campaign consultants' perceptions of what the national stage required.

Once they had concluded that California would be the make or break battleground, Borger and Hernandez launched their new "team" campaign in Riverside. The advance staff, which now included several members of the Hernandez family, promoted the event throughout the city and surrounding communities. They also arranged for buses to transport people, Hispanic voters in particular, from a number of outlying areas.

Local and national media were teased about a major, unprecedented announcement.

It was a brilliant springtime Saturday afternoon. A crowd of 3,500 to 4,000 had assembled to see and hear Borger. A mariachi band entertained them until Borger himself mounted the stage taking two steps up at a time and jumping energetically to the microphone, the audience applauding politely but with little enthusiasm.

"Good afternoon my friends. Thank you so much for coming. Before I say more, I want to introduce someone. Someone who will be campaigning right beside me the rest of the way in this crusade of ours. She recently finished two very successful terms as governor of the state just up the road there. And I know you will be as excited as I am to have her join me. I present to you Adrianna Hernandez!"

Not quite sure what was happening, the people clapped more vigorously and shouted, but appeared hesitant to release their full approval. Hernandez, dignified and confident, appeared beside Borger and accepted his one arm hug.

"Estoy muy feliz de estar contigo mis amigos. Y muy emocionado de haber venido aquí para apoyar a Wallace Borger para que sea nominado para presidente de los Estados Unidos."

Now they cheered with gusto, a roar that washed over her almost physically, almost frightening. They did not hear her repeat the words in English. When she continued again in Spanish her voice was drowned in chants of "Adrianna. Adrianna." Glancing at Borger for some sign of what to do she saw only a benevolent smile, clapping hands, and nodding head. Only by motioning for quiet could she bring the noise level down enough to finish her speech.

The event splashed across television news and internet sites, along with pundits crawling over each other to speculate whether Borger already had picked his nominee for vice president and, if so, what it meant. This would be an unprecedented move, some explained expertly. A calculated maneuver with great risk, others said. He would be resting his chance for nomination on an inexperienced Hispanic woman. Not likely to make up the lost ground. Will be seen as desperate. Not now. Country's not ready.

Borger and Hernandez reveled in the attention, good and bad. The campaign suddenly attracted mega media coverage, far more than Borger alone had enjoyed. The press corps followed the bus convoy as they passed through Orange and Los Angeles Counties, stopping for short speeches in Santa Ana, Anaheim, Long Beach, Compton, Watts, and downtown LA, before stopping for the night at a downtown hotel where they held a brief, impromptu press conference, and ate dinner with several potential sources of money.

The convoy resumed early the next morning. Following US 101. Thousand Oaks. Oxnard. Santa Barbara. Lear jet to San Luis Obispo, then Monterey for more meetings while the buses caught up.

Enormous crowds waited in Salinas and Watsonville for "La Latina Famosa". More huge rallies in San Jose and Oakland. The unconventional campaign dominated the weekend news programs. Spencer and Wright made a bet about how many times Borger or Hernandez would be asked if he already had picked her for the ticket. Both underestimated the number by at least 50.

The media production group used video and sound clips from the weekend road trip to create two powerful television commercials, each featuring Hernandez as much, if not a bit more, than Borger. One piece showed Borger delivering one of his standard deliberately stated phrases then fading into a dramatic close-up shot of Hernandez passionately exclaiming a call to action in Spanish with English subtitles appearing at the bottom of the screen. The camera then zoomed out across the heads of a multitude cheering wildly. The commercial ended with this phrase in bright blue letters: "If you want a leader like Adrianna Hernandez you must vote for Wallace Borger". It would run throughout California multiple times each day until the primary, which, as the campaign stopped in Sacramento and headed north, was seven days off.

Belatedly realizing what a Borger victory in California could do to his juggernaut push for the nomination, Mike Jordan revised his schedule and flew into LAX with a flourish and a nine-point lead in the polls. Immediately upon arriving he chided the media for focusing so much attention on his opponent. I respect Mr. Borger very much, he said, but the country right now needs new ideas, new directions, new energy. Someone who has been around among the established powers as long as Mr. Borger has just cannot provide them.

The press duly carried his message to its audience. However, some wondered why he did not mention the new factor – indeed the new force -- in Borger's corner.

Jordan, who previously had declined to debate live with Borger, now called for one to be arranged before the primary. It is too late, he was told. Distorting this to be Borger's refusal, Jordan fastened on it like a mad dog with its jaw locked in flesh. It is very telling, he told one group after another, that Mr. Borger will not debate with me. What is he afraid of?

To which Borger affably replied: "I would be most happy to debate Mr. Jordan. I call on him to name the date, time, and place." Of course, Borger well knew it was not possible. And Jordan daily grew more exasperated. And the polls daily reported the margin narrowing.

Until the day arrived and Borger celebrated a victory with Hernandez by his side. He gave her ample credit.

Momentum propelled the campaign through the remaining primaries. Still Borger insisted again and again that

Hernandez had not been selected as his VP candidate. The more they appeared together for appearance after appearance, however, and as new commercials rolled out featuring Borger in the leading role and Hernandez consistently in a supporting one, the press began to detect and report a wink of the eye whenever Borger responded on the subject.

Jordan continued his determined fight for the nomination. Apparently taking a cue from his opponent's tactics, he appeared with various other political celebrities who proclaimed their support, after which Jordan would remark about what a splendid vice president the person would make.

The two televised debates between the candidates helped Jordan more than Borger.   Almost unanimously the commentators deemed Jordan the debate victor.   He was aggressive and suave, served up memorable phrase bits, and exuded supreme confidence. Borger, on the other hand, was his usual too thoughtful self. The voters are not electing an intellect, one pundit wagged.

Borger also was without his not-so-secret weapon. If only Adrianna Hernandez could debate Jordan, some supporters mumbled wistfully.

So when the national convention opened at the Staples Center in Los Angeles Jordan held a slim lead in committed delegates, although at least 75 short of the number needed for nomination. His people worked the floor, lobby, and hotel suites with classic personal pressure style to persuade the approximately 110 uncommitted. Their primary angle was "you know Borger cannot possibly win in November".

Borger's strategy, on the other hand, was much different. He instructed everyone associated with his campaign not to beg or cajole. He would await the decision without applying any more pressure on the process. Holding court in his suite, he lavished attention on anyone who visited, and introduced them to Hernandez who presided with him like a political princess. But he would do no more.

Except ask Hernandez to give the first nominating speech.

At five foot seven she appeared like a tiny toy figure stepping to the platform, until the giant video screens flashing around the arena were filled by a bright image of her smiling face sometimes laughing at the wonderful euphoria exploding before her. Twenty, thirty, forty thousand heads shouting into a sustained roar that overwhelmed her auditory system and generated powerful punches of adrenalin. The people seemed to surge forward like an ocean tide, hands reaching for her from 50 feet away.

Ten minutes passed before she could be heard. "Mis amigos," she tried to say. "My friends—" Only to be drowned in the clamorous chaos. Eventually, after waving for quiet many times, she was able to continue. "Mis amigos, estoy aquí para nominar un hombre extraordinario para presidente de los Estados Unidos. An extraordinary man. A man we are blessed to have with us, on our side. De nuestro lado amigos!"

Now a small group somewhere out there was chanting "Adrianna. Adrianna." Barely audible up front.

Hernandez continued, hitting the issues that were important to her and explaining how Borger was the only candidate who had the wisdom to effect positive change. Without mentioning Jordan by name, she asked which of Borger's opponents for the nomination have offered anything but platitudes and meaningless promises.

"Adrianna. Adrianna." More scattered voices joining the chorus.

"This party cannot afford to pass by the opportunity before it. There is only one man for the job, one man who has the intelligence, the vision, the decisiveness to move this country forward into a future that will benefit all of our citizens, not just a privileged few. Un hombre que trabajará para todos Americanos, incluyendo personas como tu y yo. Ese hombre es – this man is Wallace Borger and I am proud and privileged to nominate him as this party's choice for president of the United States."

The customary demonstration erupted: giant placards moving up and down the aisles, balloons cascading from the rafters, horns blaring, spotlights blasting. Hernandez and assembled politicos clapping above it all and now trying to inspire a different chant: "Vive Borger. Vive Borger."

Which the crowd took up for a few minutes. Before another chant competed for attention: "Adrianna. Adrianna."

The morning before balloting was to begin the campaign sent a promotional video to all the television outlets. Hernandez introduced it, saying "Wallace Borger is not your ordinary politician. While his opponents are grubbing for votes at the convention, what is he doing? Let's take a look."

Among other scenes, it showed Borger playing basketball with a couple of older men wearing Lakers jerseys and a number of young Hispanic and black men at a neighborhood outdoor court somewhere in south Los Angeles. The clip consisted of him running the length of the court, receiving a full court pass, making a lay-up, and distributing high fives all around.

The successful candidate would need 1788 delegate votes to secure the nomination. During the first ballot 1731 votes were cast for Jordan, 1263 for Borger, and 581 spread among four other candidates, including two favorite sons. For the first time in the lives of many delegates the convention would need a second ballot, if not more.

The network commentators played it up. "I have heard it from several sources in the Jordan campaign that this is quite a surprise. Apparently they expected to go over the top by 50 or 60 votes. We have not seen this kind of drama at a convention in decades."

"Needless to say, people on both campaigns are working feverishly to woo some of those 581 and particularly to convince Governor Andrews and Senator Dworkin to release their delegates."

"I just saw Adrianna Hernandez huddling with Andrews and members of the Texas delegation. Will she make a difference here as she did in the competition leading up to the convention?"

"Here is the scene outside Mike Jordan's suite. Pandemonium. Aides holding the doors open as a constant stream of people are seen going in and coming out. One thing I have noticed – and this may mean something, or it may mean nothing – many of the delegates going in to talk with the candidate I recognize as already committed Jordan delegates. Not sure if he's trying to hold them or using them as messengers or what –"

"Sorry to interrupt you. But we just got word that Governor Andrews has released his delegates and that most, if not all, of Texas is going over to Borger."

Second ballot: 1703 for Jordan. 1397 for Borger. 475 for others.

Borger clearly has momentum. Will it be enough? Can Jordan stop the bleeding? It is past midnight here in Los Angeles. Fatigue may be a factor.

Third ballot: 1652 for Jordan. 1615 for Borger. 308 for others.

Rampant rumors that the next one will do it. Everyone is exhausted. Except apparently for Adrianna Hernandez, who is still working the floor with remarkable energy.

Fourth ballot: 1848 for Borger. Followed by the chair recognizing a Jordan representative who said the candidate had asked him to move for Borger's nomination to be made unanimous. It was done.

Borger wasted no time in making it official: Adrianna

Hernandez would be joining the ticket as candidate for vice president.

Their opponents for the general election were former vice president George Merriman and the two-term junior senator from Idaho, Herbert Young. In the first week of September the polls had Merriman-Young with a high single digit lead over Borger-Hernandez.

The latter's campaign strategists now grappled with a difficult decision: Should the candidates continue the appearances duet that had been so successful thus far? Or should they each campaign separately so as to cover more ground?

The eventual plan, for better or worse, was to work a kind of hybrid. For the first half of September they appeared together at several high-profile events, set up to generate maximum media coverage. Then Borger stepped back from the fray to project a more august aura, of one who already is deliberating on how he will address the nation's critical needs, as if he already was the president-elect. He appeared to the people principally by electronic communications – via social media, online video, television interviews, and, during the last two weeks of October, debates.

Meanwhile Hernandez campaigned the old-fashioned way. Seven, eight, nine speeches a day. Grabbing thousands of hands. Kissing babies. Eating barbequed pigs feet, chorizos, and disgusting corn dogs.

Almost every day some elderly Hispanic lady approached and said "Senora Hernandez, estoy muy feliz de que seas nuestro próximo presidente." Each time Hernandez made certain to correct the lady: "No no. Senor Borger será el presidente si ganamos, si Dios quiere. Seré vice-presidente."

Even though she was exhausted by the very late hours, was able to sleep only for a few hours, and became more worn and weary as the days of October passed, and even though she daily faced some miscreant citizens who took upon themselves to "put her in her place" by spewing verbal abuse concerning her gender, her ethnicity, her affinity for immigrants, and sometimes even her policy opinions, she loved campaigning.   The confrontations toughened her. And the overwhelming love she attracted from the rest of those who came to see her buoyed her to a height of jubilation she had never thought achievable.

One incident tested her mettle dramatically. And her capacity for leadership. Because she mingled fearlessly with the people her secret service protectors often grew very nervous and tense.   On one occasion, in Spokane, Washington, as she was moving through a crowd outside the Veterans Memorial Arena following a speech, three young men with shaved heads, dressed in camouflage gear, suddenly appeared up close, shouting "Go back where you came from Mexican bitch!" and spitting on the ground by her feet.

Even before she could react, two agents stepped between her and the men, drew their weapons, and thrust the barrels up under the chins of the two closest.   "Give me an excuse motherfucker," one of the agents said.   Now believing that Hernandez had been assaulted, several of her supporters in the crowd attacked the men, knocking them down, and kicking them furiously.

Once she realized what was happening, Hernandez pulled both agents back forcefully, pushed through the bodies until she was standing over the men cowering on the ground.   "Stop. Stop," she cried, and waved for the people to stand back, suggesting by her pose that the next blow would strike her before it did anyone else.

Clearly on the verge of outright crying, she stifled the urge, and helped the stunned young men stand up. They stared at her in terrified disbelief.

"This is not how we do it in America," she shouted.

"These 'boys' are as wrong as can be. But in America, in Spokane, Washington, they have the right to be wrong and the right to let everyone know how wrong they are. As long as they do not cause harm to anyone. They did not cause any harm to me with their pathetic and stupid words. So let them be on their way." Waving them off, the three disappeared. And the crowd transformed from an angry mob into a jubilant congregation, chanting "Adrianna. Adrianna."

Videos of the incident proliferated throughout the internet and television networks, some of which sensationalized it shamelessly. Calls and messages came in by the hundreds. Borger and most of the staff were very upset and somewhat angry at her for risking her safety. That's what the secret service is there for, they complained. Neither their admonishments, however, nor any of the general furor elicited any response from Hernandez.

News and talk show producers clamored for interviews. Hernandez refused all such invitations if there was to be any discussion of the incident. She would only discuss issues salient to the election. Otherwise she went on with her schedule.

But it became quickly obvious that the campaign had been transformed into a new level. She was no longer drawing "running mate" crowds. The People turned out in enormous numbers, dwarfing any that had come to see previous VP candidates. And they were wildly enthusiastic. So much so that she had great difficulty speaking about Borger. Whenever she tried the chant would crescendo at her like a giant wave of sound: "Adrianna. Adrianna." It was, as the press now characterized it, a phenomenon.

Rumors and speculation surrounded the campaign's headquarters. Borger was so exasperated by the development, the stories went, that he was exploring how to part ways with Hernandez. Then it turned out that Borger was not bothered at all, that the anxiety was coming from some of his top aides, who worried nonsensically about what would happen if a candidate for vice president received more votes than the man at the top. "Any candidate would love to have this problem", Borger quipped in response to press questions as he proceeded to a vigorous run through Central Park.

By the last week of October the polls reported no statistically meaningful gap between the candidates.

Both Merriman and Young were campaigning relentlessly. And growing visibly spent. The two presidential debates were dull and decidedly uncontentious. Neither candidate emerged the proclaimed victor.

Young's campaign canceled the one scheduled VP debate unilaterally with the pretext that the two sides could not agree on the procedures to be followed. However, this dispute occurred only because Young's people belatedly demanded new, patently unacceptable procedures four days before the date. While Hernandez remained graceful in her attitude about the matter, her more prominent supporters loudly declared it obvious that Young was afraid to debate her.

To close out the campaign Borger and Hernandez planned a whirlwind tour through ten states for the final three days before election day. At each stop they reprised their pre-primary dual appearance program, except that Hernandez spoke first and introduced Borger.

In their nightcap meeting after the first day the campaign staff unanimously proclaimed it a great success. Atlanta, Charlotte, Nashville, Scranton, Cleveland, and Indianapolis. Hernandez' popularity continuing to surge, she had addressed tremendously excited crowds and aroused them into a frenzy that carried over for Borger. Borger then showed extraordinary vigor bounding to center stage and speaking with uncharacteristic gusto. He finally went to bed at 1:30 a.m., visibly weary, but still buzzing with adrenalin.

They started the next morning at 8:30 a.m. in Chicago. The energy continued where it had left off the night before. As the candidates were about to take the stage Two new polls reported showed them pulling slightly ahead, immediately dispelling some remaining fatigue that had slightly slowed Borger.

By their fifth stop of the day, however, in Des Moines, after Detroit, Milwaukie, and Minneapolis, Borger was no longer bounding forward. Instead he approached a few steps at a time, waving as he made his way. His speech weakened and he began to rest an arm on the shoulder of an aide.

"Running out of gas?" someone asked him privately. "Nonsense", he replied with exaggerated conviction.

But after St. Louis and Tulsa, he had to acknowledge his condition. A physician traveling among the entourage interviewed him about his symptoms, diagnosed him with severe exhaustion, and recommended immediate bedrest. A slight touch of the flu was the diagnosis casually leaked to the press. He just needed to rest and slow down his schedule.

The formal announcement stated that he would rest for the remainder of the day and resume the campaign schedule in the morning. Meanwhile, Hernandez would continue on alone, appearing solo for all the events scheduled later that day.

Any fear that Borger's absence would hurt the turnout evaporated as the tour stopped in Albuquerque, Denver, Boise, and finally Salt Lake City. There seemed no reduction in either the size or enthusiasm of the crowds. Hernandez spoke about Borger as earnestly and passionately as she could, but each time her exhortations only prompted the familiar chant: "Adrianna. Adrianna." As gratifying as it was, she hoped Borger's close companions were preventing him from watching the spectacle on television.

Hernandez herself was worn out when she collapsed into

a luxurious stuffed chair in her hotel suite. After talking briefly with her husband and children over the phone, she called the suite Borger had taken in Oklahoma City. It was 10:30.

"Adrianna Hernandez. Can I talk with the old man?"

"He is asleep. Better call back in the morning."

"Well tell me how he's doing. I have not been updated for about three hours."

"Not sure. Dr. Venable is here. Flew in from New York."

"So it's more serious than we thought? Can I talk to Venable?"

"I would say yes, but I don't know the details. Dr. Venable is on the phone. Consulting with someone I think."

"Can you just tell me this: Will he be able to join me in the morning as planned?"

"Doubt it."

"Please be sure I am informed. No matter what time it is."

"Of course, Ms. Hernandez."

Needing sleep desperately, she sent everyone out and laid down. But it quickly proved to be impossible. Too much anxiety. Nerves already buzzing from the coming day of truth only day after tomorrow. Now amped even more. So many scenarios unfolding in her mind. News or rumors of a sick candidate firing across the firmament. What if it's a long illness? Hospital?

Turning on the television. "At least one source, don't know how reliable, is reporting that Wallace Borger's condition may be more than just exhaustion. No word from the campaign. I mean no word. One way or the other. Not even a no comment."

Newly alarmed. Calling Borger's suite again. Same person. Hernandez angry: "I want to know what the hell is going on there. Don't want to hear it from CNN!"

"Yes, of course Ms. Hernandez. But Mr. Borger is not here. Dr. Venable had him taken to St Anthony hospital nearby. For observation I understand."

"And when in God's name was I going to be informed?"

"Gosh, I'm sorry Ms. Hernandez. I don't know who is handling that."

Fumbling to put on a robe as she burst into the anteroom. Two staff members quickly hiding cell phones, their distraught faces barely disguising frantic agitation. Staring at her. Afraid. Like she had a gun and was intending to use it.

She realized instantly that they knew something she did not. "What's going on?" she said, taut and tense and fighting tears.

"What do you mean?" one them weakly responded.

She could feel her face flaming. Shouting like she never had before: "Tell me or I'll have you both fired and thrown into the street. Or maybe I'll do it myself." Approaching them. Menacing glare.

Instead of telling her the truth they started babbling about why they hadn't. "They told us not to say anything to you. That you did not need to know yet. That you needed to rest."

Hands gripping hips. Fury tears moistening her eyes. Speaking without breathing. "Tell .. me .. what?"

One of them squeaked: "He's gone."

Confusion. "What do you mean 'he's gone'?"

"He's dead." And the other: "Heart attack."

The shock struck her full force between the eyes. For a long moment she was suspended before them like a boxer who has been knocked out but net yet fallen. Unable to grasp it. Unwilling to grasp it. Desperately searching her mind for an explanation that would solve this impossible event. That would allow her to return to her room, go to sleep, wake up, and hit the campaign trail again as she had for so many days past, Wallace Borger with her, on his way to becoming president-elect the next day.

But then, as if it were a narrator's gloomy voiceover in a

documentary, the news floated over from a television left on somewhere in the room: "This is a special report ... CNN has just received an unconfirmed report – I repeat .. unconfirmed – that presidential candidate Wallace Borger is on life support in an Oklahoma City hospital after an apparent heart attack. The report says that Borger had been taken to the hospital earlier for observation after he was said to be suffering exhaustion. There is no word yet ..."

Her self-control finally released; Hernandez began to sob even as she tried to hide it by holding her hands to her face. One of the two freaked out staffers scurried away to the comfort of his cell phone. The other turned off the television. The secret service agent on duty dragged a chair over and gently bent her into it.

Her husband, when he called after hearing the news, trying to comfort and listening to her blubber about losing a father: "What happens now to the campaign?"

Snapping viciously: "What do you think happens to the campaign! Nothing! It's over! You can't figure that out!"

"Sorry. I just thought that –"

"Forget it! I'll talk to you tomorrow." Crying even harder after disconnecting.

Someone brought her a glass of water. "I don't want water, damn it. Get me a drink!" No one had ever heard her use this language. No one had ever seen her drink.

But she did. And eventually stopped crying. And fell asleep.

4

Hernandez awakened at 4:30 a.m. mountain time. She immediately asked if Borger had in fact died or was still on life support. A campaign heavy who had been assigned to "take care" of her told her that his latest intelligence indicated Borger was still breathing.

"Can I go see him?"

"No, that is impossible."

"Why?"

"Sorry ma'am, I do not know. My orders are that you cannot see Mr. Borger and that I am to escort you to the airport for a flight to Tucson."

"Who gave those orders?"

"I don't know, but they came from the top."

"From Borger?"

"I don't know ma'am. But I doubt it."

Exhausted despite the sleep, weak and still in some shock, Hernandez did not have the will to dispute the "orders". She probably would not have in any event; what would be the point, since even if Borger was being kept alive artificially there was nothing she could do and, grim as the thought was, his functional life clearly had ended.

As had her prospect for becoming vice president. She might as well go home.

Deciding that any public appearance or statement would be disrespectful, she exited the plane at Tucson International, traversed the executive terminal, and disappeared in a black Mercedes without once parting the dark blue veil shrouding her face. Cousins, uncles, and secret service had cleared a path into her home and there she stayed for the next 48 hours.

Calls for a public statement reached her from inside and outside the campaign. She refused. A few brave souls broached with her the subject of next moves in her career, only to see her shake her head and mutter "not now please". Only close family and friends were allowed in the home. A ring of "protectors" circled the property, growling at reporters and threatening to beat any who dared try to penetrate.

Chaos and confusion captured the morning news. Anchors and correspondents grappled with an overwhelming flow of stunningly conflicting reports. Borger is dead. He passed at around 1:30 in the morning. Borger is not dead. He is in extremely critical condition and still on life support. Borger is recovering. He should be out of the hospital later in the day.

The hospital made no official announcement, which only intensified the drama. Access to the floor where Borger was last known to have been taken was blocked by men in dark suits, sunglasses, and communication device wires dangling from their ears. Secret service? If so, Borger must still be alive. Why would they be guarding a corpse?

Every hospital employee leaving the building was accosted and harassed by reporters demanding to hear what he or she knew. Every answer was the same: Borger was brought to the hospital shortly before midnight and admitted to the ICU. What has happened since? No clue.

No press people, who had been laying siege to the hospital, with battle lines increasing since midnight, had seen anything resembling a body bag or a coffin or any other receptacle that might carry a body. Nor had anyone seen members of Borger's family enter the hospital.

Borger's daughter issued a cryptic statement from Madison, Wisconsin, where she is a professor of law, pleading for the press and the public generally to respect the family's privacy and hinting that they would consider legal action if necessary, but saying nothing about whether Borger was alive or dead. Did she simply assume that everyone already knew he was dead? If so, there would have been no reason to mention it. So he must be dead.

Everyone understands and respects the family's desire for privacy, went the somewhat hysterical response, but it is a matter of urgent national importance and probably security to know what Mr. Borger's condition is. How can people vote intelligently if they don't know whether their candidate is alive or about to die or dead already?

Intelligently or not, the voting had to begin. It was too late to call it off. Ballots were printed and programmed. The machinery was loaded and ready to roll. Poll watchers had been assigned. Get out the vote groups were geared up for action. Television and internet networks had squads, even armies, of personnel poised at the frontlines and batteries of pundits locked into studio chairs. The election had to proceed -- as if Borger himself, trapped in an intermediate nether world, was awaiting the outcome before he could proceed to his final destination.

Political commentators vied with each other to say something more vacuous than the others. "If Borger has died this is an unprecedented situation," they declared. "No nominated major party candidate for president ever has died before the election." Something even most middle school students already knew.

Possible consequences of potential developments were sketched by multitudes of pretentious egos calling themselves political, constitutional, historical, or legal experts. There were protracted dissertations on the non-constitutional status of political parties and their nominees. Which meant that the death of a candidate would not affect the process as prescribed by the founders, and tweaked by amendment, and thus that the election could proceed with only one major eligible candidate on the ballot, the other name representing a candidate who was not eligible because he was dead. No one appeared on a major network to ask why a dead person would not be eligible.

On the other hand, some wondered what the effect of the Twentieth Amendment would be if Borger were declared brain dead but kept alive by the power of medical technology. Most commentators, however, pronounced such speculation a huge waste of their time and fell back on the critical need to discover the facts. The hospital or the family – somebody – must come forward with definitive word.

Yet no official at the hospital would speak. So at 1:30 p.m. central time a battalion of lawyers arrived at the United States District Court for the Western District of Oklahoma in Oklahoma City to petition for an emergency injunction compelling the hospital, or any other appropriate agency, to provide up to date information on Borger's condition.

Lawyers for the hospital, the Borger campaign, the family, various medical associations, and ad hoc privacy advocates also appeared. All there to oppose the petition, those who actually were able to speak argued that no cause for an injunction existed because there was no credible evidence of any actual or threatened harmful conduct – no evidence, for example, that Borger had died and that someone was concealing this information. Your honor cannot issue an injunction based only on rumors.

The judge denied the petition on the ground that, on the record before her, she did not have the power to compel anyone to disclose private information that was not being wrongfully concealed. If proof of any such conduct emerges it will need to be addressed after the fact, in other words, after the election. The losing group moved on to the Tenth Circuit Court of Appeals, which was just as unhelpful.

As afternoon of election eve wore on most commentators concluded that the issue probably had become moot anyway. With Borger dead or dying, it was clear that George Merriman was going to be elected president and Herbert Young vice president. Of course, they said, some people, maybe a lot of people, will vote Borger and Hernandez out of sentiment, but many more would simply not cast a wasted vote.

In fact, the tragedy would not be limited to the

presidential race. How many would-be Borger voters will not vote at all, they lamented, which will have a disastrous impact on state and local races all down the ballot. This certainly will be the most aberrant and tumultuous election since 1860. Untangling the resulting mess was certain to be an extraordinarily complicated, contentious, and bitter process, perhaps even destructive or violent, as the aftermath of 1860 proved to be.

Election day. The most depressing one in anyone's memory. An ugly pall seemed to hang in the air like toxic smoke all over the country. A frightening sense of doom pervaded the people.

Yet still they trekked to the polls. By around 2:30 eastern time shocking reports of tremendous turnouts had emanated from various news outlets. Commentators increasingly consternated. "We're getting accounts of long lines at some polling places in the largest eastern urban districts".

The first real sign of an astonishing trend was reflected in the strained effort of network television news reporters to pretend that the exit polls had yet to reveal anything significant, lest decisive information should leak out before the polls closed. Anchors brought them on air with the banal "what are we learning from the exit polls?" The typical response was "it's pretty hard to tell yet" and "our information is coming in somewhat chaotically" and "we are having trouble verifying some of the results". Again the only fact that could be announced as confirmed was that turn-out had been, and continued to be, very heavy.

Even when polls had closed in some states, the time the networks expected to begin projecting Merriman as the winner in state after state, the news blabber instead was remarkably vague, almost evasive. The correspondents seemed reluctant to state anything as definite, as if they believed that the reports coming in might be false and that nothing should be said without extra confirmation.

It was not until 9:30 eastern time that one network ventured to declare a winner in one state. The announcement was prefaced with hyperbole about how incredible the information was, but that it had been confirmed multiple times. "So we are compelled to project that Wallace Borger will win in South Carolina. And that his margin of victory will be substantial."

Equally surprising projections followed, giving a few states to Merriman, but many more to Borger. By midnight eastern time it was over. The networks unanimously projected Wallace Borger, dead or not, as the winner. However, none went so far as to label him the president-elect.

Now the exit polls provided some insight into the extraordinary results. A curious trend had been emerging throughout the night, but only gained serious attention once the delayed projections were announced one after another in an unprecedented short time period. It seemed also that the most telling questions were not asked of voters until the Borger vote phenomenon had become evident. At some point thereafter exit poll troops began to ask of Borger voters, specifically and pointedly, three questions:

1. Are you aware that Wallace Borger is either dead or on life support?
2. Do you believe that Wallace Borger is still alive?
3. Why did you vote for Wallace Borger?

The overwhelming answer to the first question was yes. Answers to the second question came in at a consistent ratio of one in five saying yes and the other four saying I don't know.

Results for the third question astounded those who professed to view them objectively. When answers from those few who had responded no to the first question were excluded, the results were roughly summarized as follows:

15 percent: Great respect for Borger, dead or alive;

12 percent: Intense dislike for Merriman or believe he is dishonest and corrupt;

19 percent: Miscellaneous reasons; and

54 percent: If Borger is dead or cannot serve Hernandez will be president.

So the American people woke up Wednesday morning not knowing whether they had elected a president or a ghost. After a trying day fending off inquiries and unsuccessfully begging for information about Borger's condition, Hernandez finally willed herself into equanimity and decided she would live for the next hour and the next and the ones that followed as if Borger was yet alive and president-elect of the United States.

Which meant that she was vice president-elect. But she did not feel it. Neither did the zombies moving around her home mumbling meaningless sentence fragments Only the children, seeing their mother and aunt so distraught and distracted, were able to break through the hypnotic haze and approach to hug her, which warmed her and calmed her anxiety, at least for a few minutes.

A decision was made, not by Hernandez, who nonetheless acquiesced in it, to shut off all media devices that could not be filtered so as to prevent any of the madness echoing across the airwaves and through the electronic ether from reaching her. She and those closest to her would wait for the word -- that was sure to come and that was certain to be unequivocally urgent.

At 11:45 a.m. the landline phone rang for the 777th time that day. A designated assistant answered. Every other time this person had told the caller either "Ms. Hernandez is not available" or "you will need to speak with someone at the – about that" or "I will need to hang up now". This time the person said "Please hold on. I will check", walked to a small office outside the room where Hernandez was trying to rest, and said to the assistant stationed there: "It's Patty Borger." Borger's law professor daughter.

Hernandez took the call.

"Hello Patty."

"Adrianna, it is so good to finally hear your voice." Somber and sullen.

"I've been here."

"I know and I am so so sorry that you have been kept in the dark. It just seemed the only way."

"Well Patty, I am so sorry about your father."

"Thank you. It has been an ordeal to say the least." Tension tightening the voice. Great emotion controlled.

Hernandez waited for the news, the silence loud and pulsing.

"Adrianna ... he's gone." Slow sobs choked off.

"Oh no! ... When?"

"The final word came about 30 minutes ago. Not sure when the end .." More sobbing. "I wasn't there. He was peaceful. Heart beating. No other signs. They said it could go on like that. I had to go. Could not take it." Overcome by weeping, trying to breathe.

Hernandez covered her face with one hand while the other held the phone. Looking into a dark abyss. Struggling to grasp the reality. Suddenly rising before her a monstrous monolithic gravestone blocking out all that had been just moments before. The inscription chiseled prominent and solid across it: "*IF, AT THE TIME FIXED FOR THE BEGINNING OF THE TERM OF THE PRESIDENT, THE PRESIDENT ELECT SHALL HAVE DIED, THE VICE PRESIDENT ELECT SHALL BECOME PRESIDENT.*"

"Adrianna, you now are the president elect. God help you."

5

The result of the election has not become clear to everyone's satisfaction. Borger is indeed dead. A corpse purporting to be his was displayed in the Minnesota capitol rotunda for a two-day viewing. And all the actors in the ensuing drama acted on the assumption that at least as of the morning after the election he was dead.

Some controversy, however, arose from the absence of any official report as to the exact time of death. A subdued controversy to be sure. Only a handful of media rascals mentioned the matter publicly. No one with any official capacity in either party or the incumbent administration dared to speak about it before the final services and burial of Boger had concluded in St. Cloud, Minnesota.

The funeral attracted massive attention, not only because of the tragic and momentous circumstances, but more because of the extraordinary harmony and fellowship that prevailed. Leaders of both parties, including the president, Merriman, Young, and of course Hernandez, attended. All the partisan animosity that had fouled the campaign gave way to rampant hugging and tears and benevolent gestures.

Also, until Borger was safely interred, and the final eulogy pronounced, no person with any standing to do so had challenged Hernandez' claim to the presidency under the 20th Amendment. Not that she personally made the claim. She never uttered a public word about it. But hosts of supporters did. From the morning Borger's demise was announced a general proclamation, spoken and unspoken, positive yet somber and respectful, had issued from the People, the press, the pundits, politicos, and popular culture personalities, recognizing as an accomplished fact Hernandez' succession to the title of President-elect.

Although fearfully reluctant to act the part, and to do what a president-to-be-in-January must do beginning in November, Hernandez was bombarded by supplicants for places in her administration. She also received a constant, overloading stream of advice. Her known email addresses were glutted and disabled by an overwhelming mass of electronically transmitted wisdom and offers of "expert" assistance. Multiple bags of paper mail were delivered every day.

It was almost as if everyone in America assumed that Hernandez, because she was relatively inexperienced and had not planned to become president, needed their help to prepare for governing the nation. Perhaps some also believed that she needed more help than past presidents-elect because of her sex.

It is not certain that Hernandez would have successfully navigated through the two months following the election if it had not been for the invaluable dedication and capability of her sister, Jenny. Jumping into the role of unofficial chief of staff, Jenny quickly set up shop in an office suite leased from a real estate broker friend of the family. She hired staff to handle matters she could not manage herself. She composed and distributed press releases, most of which simply bought time and space for the boss to spend figuring out what the heck she needed to do. She created and registered websites that served as receptors and repositories for the vast quantities of communications coming in.

The rest of the very extended family also contributed to the process, each doing whatever he or she could to alleviate the pressure on Hernandez. However, she became angry whenever it was revealed to her that someone had missed school or work to help. "I won't have it!" she announced. "I will quit the whole thing if anyone in my family is harmed in any way, however slightly it may seem."

The hastily assembled "transition team" included many of Borger's campaign staff who volunteered to help coordinate transfer of power with the incumbent office holders and to continue the media partnership that had come to such a successful fruition on the eve of the election. This help, however, was motivated by the general assumption that Hernandez would carry out the plans and policies that Borger had intended to implement, that she would adopt the role essentially of an "acting" president, and not pursue much of her own, independent agenda. She chose not to disabuse anyone of this assumption before she took office.

When the gloom had dissipated, and the national anxiety was more controlled, disgruntled Merriman people began to voice questions about the legitimacy of the result. Their queries centered on whether Borger had truly been elected, and thus had been the "president-elect", within the meaning of the 20th Amendment.

The exact time of death was critical, they argued. If Borger was dead before election day, he could not have been eligible, and votes cast for him would be null and void.   Even if he was essentially brain dead and kept alive with artificial life support, that condition would also disqualify him. Hernandez cannot be sworn in as president unless and until there is adequate proof that Borger was still living with a functioning brain, as of some to be determined hour on election day. They called for an immediate congressional investigation.

Merriman himself ducked the issue. Following the funeral he flew with his family to an undisclosed ski resort somewhere in Canada and let others heat up the pot. He did allow release of a statement agreeing that proof of the time of death would be helpful.

More vociferous objectors labeled the succession of Hernandez a preposterous abuse of the 20th Amendment. That provision, they contended, in no way required the elevation of a *candidate* for vice-president in the circumstances presented here. The framers of the amendment could not conceivably have contemplated applying it where the election results had not even been certified or delivered to Congress. Most of these malcontents wanted the House of Representatives to determine the outcome.

The hospital in Oklahoma City diffused the clamor arising around the time of death issue by releasing a statement explaining that Borger's physician, Dr. Venable, had pronounced him deceased at 9:43 a.m. local time on the day following the election. While not placating those who wanted detailed facts about Borger's condition over the 48 hours before the death pronouncement, to answer the brain dead/life support question, the statement quelled the leading cries for an investigation. With no other official action likely, the questioning settled into a debate that excited only commentators and academics.

The constitutional construction issue enjoyed a longer, more vigorous life. In fact, it has not yet been resolved; although it will not stop the inauguration of Hernandez. The difficulty in challenging the constitutional legitimacy of a Hernandez presidency is that there apparently is no body with power to do anything about it. There have been several lawsuits launched, and ingenious theories to support them. However, no court so far has found that it can either adjudicate the issue or order a remedy. No one has acted or failed to act such that a prohibitory or mandatory injunction can have any effect. Hernandez herself is not attempting to take the presidency from someone who has rightfully been chosen for it.

And, be that circumstance as it may, none of the courts that have proffered dicta addressing the substantive question have found any reason to impose a different construction of the 20th Amendment. The People clearly chose Borger to be their president and Hernandez to be vice-president. Then Borger died. The constitution provides no means other than the amendment for determining who will be installed in his place.

So Adrianna Hernandez will be inaugurated as the first female and first Hispanic President of the United States.

6

It did not take long for big trouble to strike the Hernandez administration.   A thunderbolt no one expected, least of all Hernandez herself. Like a tornado suddenly exploding in the Arizona desert and charging across the desert toward Tucson. And it did not involve the death of Borger.

For three weeks euphoria replaced the gloom and uncertainty that followed in the wake of that tragic event. Hernandez brought the warm southwest sun to Washington for her inauguration. Along with mariachi bands, folkorico dancers, Latin Grammy winners, and the Reverend Ricardo Valbueno from St. Augustine Cathedral in Tucson, who gave the benediction entirely in Spanish.

A throng of Hernandez family members – some bigots called it a "horde" – also attended. Her husband and children orbited her at close range wherever she went and actually stood beside her as she delivered her speech, her daughter wearing smaller versions of the same turquoise and silver necklace and matching earrings Hernandez did. Both also appeared in bright blue dresses flecked with vermillion and yellow.

The speech, which also contained portions in Spanish, was decidedly optimistic and generally free of controversy. However, she did express strong views on two subjects: immigration and abortion, although she did not address any specific policies or programs.

Already known as very conservative in these areas, she surprised no one by declaring in favor of tighter control of entryways into the country, yet distinguished herself from past leaders by extending this need to all borders, airports, and shipping ports, not just the border with Mexico. "The greatest danger to America does not come across the border. It comes aboard airlines in the form of persons, often with false, yet facially correct, documents, who enter with ease intent on causing harm. The perpetrators of the 9/11 attacks did not come across the border!"

On abortion, she stated, as she had many times before, that her deep religious beliefs did not allow her to accept the killing of unborn children as a right under the Constitution. On the other hand, she explained, the government had neither the right nor the power to coerce women with respect to actions affecting their bodies. So, in her view, until a child was born and thus became a person separate from the mother and entitled to protection that did not affect her body, there was nothing the government could do.

Commentators uniformly agreed that the inauguration was the most festive in recent times, if not of all time. Maybe it was the very unusual balmy weather. Maybe it was the almost unprecedented bipartisan spirit. Maybe it was the advent of an extraordinarily different person as president, someone as well who had become immensely popular. "I cannot remember a time when an incoming president had so few enemies," one veteran pundit remarked. "Maybe it will not survive the turmoil of governing, but today she is making everyone feel good about the future."

This remarkable confidence continued through the following days as Hernandez settled into the daily drill of meetings, phone conferences, appearances, reviewing documents, and consulting with advisers. It seemed that political figures all over the world were clamoring for a chance to speak with her. The White House communications system was continually swamped. Within two days her established hours for in-person appointments were booked for weeks.

The first significant matter she had to address was the vacancy in the vice-president's office. The 25th Amendment provides that when the office becomes vacant the president is to nominate a new person who will then take office upon a majority vote of both houses of Congress. So Hernandez did not have the power to nominate anyone until she was inaugurated.

The choice of someone to join a ticket vying for election customarily involves considerations of political strength – what the person adds for attracting voters in a particular region of the country or among various ideology groupings. Hernandez needed to consider different factors.

Principal among them for her was the candidate's readiness and ability to assume the presidency if she did not survive. This was a major concern. Because, despite her apparent ebullience and enthusiasm, Hernandez fought a vicious internal struggle against doubt and depression. She did not believe that she would serve out the term.   Either her physical or her mental/emotional health would prevent it. Even before she took office she was contemplating her resignation. So picking the right vice-president seemed to be the most critical decision she faced, the one she absolutely had to get right.

There were a number of superb candidates. High on the list was Mike Jordan, who had fought heartily for the nomination Borger won instead. Virtually every one of Hernandez' advisers said no way. Jordan was such a star politician that he was bound to chafe at the vice-presidential constraints and to overshadow the president whenever he could. Not one to sit on the bench, some said.   Naming him vice-president would just give him the springboard to launch his next campaign. He desperately wanted to be president and there were powerful elements in the country that wanted him crowned. The threat to Hernandez' safety could not be ignored.

Of course Hernandez completely disregarded this view. Her own safety was not to be considered. And picking someone who wanted to be president actually was one of her primary objectives. Not in the least concerned about being overshadowed or bullied, she reacted to such advice by adding it to the plus column for Jordan.

Speculation that Jordan would decline the post if offered evaporated soon after he was mentioned by commentators and a couple of unnamed sources on the president's staff. "I would be very honored," he announced on a morning news show. An invitation to meet with Hernandez quickly followed. Afterwards he spoke with pointed respect for her, called her a remarkable woman, and predicted that "she will be a truly great president", whether or not she chooses him.

She did. After considering and interviewing four other high-profile candidates, she announced her choice in the East Room of the White House ten days after the inauguration. Jordan bounded to the podium with his usual energy and spoke briefly about how grateful he was to the President and how committed he was to making her administration an unprecedented success.

Through the subsequent ten days Hernandez and Jordan appeared together at multiple functions, always exuding the most congenial relationship. Jordan sat in on meetings of the cabinet and spoke to the press about issues they had discussed. Sources reported that conversations between the two sometimes grew solemn, but never acrimonious and that Hernandez generally found Jordan's input helpful, particularly concerning communications with congress.

For the first two weeks following the inauguration these communications chiefly concerned confirmation of her cabinet appointments. It was an unprecedentedly diverse group in terms of sex, race, ethnicity, and even party.

Of course many people who had worked to elect Borger expected positions in the cabinet as reward. However, Hernandez let it be known soon after the election that, while service to the campaign would be a positive factor, she intended to take several other determinants into consideration. So there was certain to be disappointment.

In the end she did ask a few Borger people to serve in the cabinet, but passed over many more. In keeping with her long-time practice of doing everything possible to avoid creating enemies, Hernandez met personally with every person who expressed the least bitterness about a perceived snub. She did not once change her decision as a result of such a meeting, and she was marginally successful at best in assuaging present bad feelings. Nonetheless, she believed that her efforts would prevent the disgruntled from harboring hostility in the long run.

However, the process was acutely wearing for her. It exhausted her spirit, which took several hours to revive.

As was the daily barrage of newly unearthed and sensationalized scandals involving one or more of the nominees. Her pick for Secretary of Agriculture reportedly had employed undocumented Costa Rican dishwashers in the restaurant chain he owned in the mid-south. She rejected advice telling her to withdraw the nomination and refused to make any public comment. It then turned out that the dishwashers were supplied by a staffing company that claimed to have obtained work visas for all its workers.

Hernandez' nominee for Commerce, a rare female entertainment mogul, was accused of sexually exploiting several aspiring male rap artists. They appeared together for news cameras at the office of a Glendale, California attorney, who recited in salacious detail how the woman had invited them to her mansion and "forced" them to have sex with her multiple times. Believing the charge false or the facts grossly misrepresented, Hernandez again declined to withdraw the pick or to speak about it. The story then unraveled when the rappers contradicted each other in their accounts of the event.

More potentially damaging were opinion pieces the selection for Treasury had published while he was a junior professor of economics at Drake University. Although too arcane for the mainstream media to analyze properly, the works were labeled by right-wing financial commentators as advocating a "pseudo communist" approach to banking and monetary policy.

Hernandez liked the guy because even though brilliant in his field, he was not arrogant like many other economics "experts" were. Quite aware that she would be judged by the progress of the economy more than any other aspect of her presidency, she determined to pursue the fiscally conservative policy she had always favored, while promoting economic programs in a manner the public could understand. To do that she needed financial and economic geniuses who appreciated the need to explain in terms people without advanced degrees – and members of Congress -- could understand.

Acknowledging the hue and cry erupting on the right, Hernandez asked the nominee to visit with her in the White House to discuss the matter. Again she had no intention of withdrawing his name, but this time the tremendous pressure applied by shrill commentators delivering salvo after salvo of vitriolic aspersions disturbed her equanimity and she hoped to dissipate it with a display of concern for the issue.

She was successful. The would-be Treasury secretary defused the controversy with self-effacing grace, explaining how his views had matured as he had and how theories filtered through experience evolve. Then, rather than disavow his earlier opinion, he demonstrated some spine by characterizing it as a limited perspective, one that looked only at a discreet segment of economic life. As such it had been useful academically, but was quite irrelevant to the work of a treasury secretary.

In the end, Congress confirmed all of Hernandez' cabinet appointments. She conducted the first meeting of the entire group in an almost celebratory atmosphere. Scorning the many idiots who warned against womanly ways softening such a solemn proceeding, she hugged everyone there, accepted kisses on the cheek from some old school gentlemen, and referred to the members as her "family". Not surprisingly, she was taken to task afterwards for lacking proper decorum and trying too hard to "lighten' up" the grim responsibilities of the president.

This jaundiced picture evaporated a few days later when she held her first press conference. Asked about the disparaging comments, Hernandez merely stared darkly at the reporter for a few moments, then said "Next question".

Asked what she hoped to accomplish on her upcoming trip to three middle eastern countries: "To assure them and the world that we stand ready to use whatever military force is necessary to maintain stability in the region". Asked whether she would wear a hijab: She again stared down the questioner, but then said icily "Absolutely not".

Asked if she expected any difficulty in dealing with leaders from countries where women are excluded from the government: "Yes. Once they hear what I will have to say they probably will not want me back." This stimulated several shouted follow-up questions. But she held her hand up and declared "No more on this subject please."

Hernandez and her husband had decided that for the first four months he and the children would remain in Tucson, so that he and they could complete their second semesters of the year as faculty and students, respectively. So loneliness became one of her major personal issues.

Her only familial presence was her sister, Jennifer, whom she appointed as a special assistant and who lived at the White House. But the president believed it important to minimize the familiarity between them, if only to bolster Jennifer's status as a genuine and independent professional.

The loneliness and anxiety she felt were fueled by the almost overwhelming sense that she did not belong there.

Adrianna Hernandez, after all, was an accidental president. She did not seek out the job. And now that she had it anyway, she had to fight off a consuming fear of failure and a potentially debilitating doubt about her desire for the enormous responsibility. She dealt with both in part by resolving to quit when the circumstances became suitable. This let her see the predicament as a short-term matter, easier to get through.

Nevertheless, she did feel a little more comfortable with each day that passed. The mornings definitely were the hardest. After sleeping fitfully, and suffering through frequent bouts of subconscious mental turmoil, she invariably awoke with horrific anxiety. She wondered how she could make it through the day. Not previously in the habit of praying, she began to call on God for help before getting out of bed and taking on the first challenge of the day.

By evening, however, she felt much calmer. A stoical numbness enveloped her thoughts, produced largely by a soothing sense that that day she had done the best she could. She certainly had made mistakes; that was inevitable for the job. But she had made decisions applying her best powers of analysis. And there was no reason to doubt whether she could do it all over again tomorrow.

Hernandez' popularity also increased each day. It seemed that the people were growing accustomed to the multiple novelties her administration featured: First woman in the office. First Hispanic. First person to assume the office on the death of a president-elect.

Not that her policies and decisions were universally praised. She did not wholly transcend the partisan divide and drew scattered objections, animosity, and rancor as did every president. But the *way* she governed pleased an extraordinary cross-section of Americans. As one commentator put it, "President Hernandez in her first weeks has brought a new aura to the White House, an aura of positivity, of respect for everyone, including those opposed to her policies. It has been said that she has a knack for disagreeing with or rejecting someone's viewpoint without making the person feel denigrated and for not creating enemies. So far she has been phenomenally successful in carrying this talent into the presidency."

So while forced to take actions that were not popular with many, Hernandez' personal image did not suffer. When a contingent of Mexicans were detained after they crossed the Texas border east of El Paso, news reports claimed that they were relatives of Hernandez. This engendered speculation as to whether she would intercede on their behalf. But her press spokesperson relayed a statement categorically dismissing any such action.

At the same time the spokesperson offered the startling suggestion that if the group could provide evidence of threats by other Mexicans to their safety or health the president would consider sending United States military units across the border, if the Mexican authorities themselves did not act promptly, to handle the matter. The outrage of those authorities notwithstanding, the statement was deemed magnificent by a large majority of Americans and quieted those who called the president's refusal to help her family shameful.

Perhaps nothing contributed to the people's love for Hernandez so much as her personal courage. Although a president's courage is tested every day, he or she holds the office, some days, some incidents are more frightening than others. Secret service agents, of course, swarmed Hernandez everywhere she went outside the White House. They also escorted her children and her husband to their schools and hovered nearby through the day. Nevertheless, she knew as everyone else did that if someone determined to hurt one of them, and was eager to die in the process, stopping him would be virtually impossible.

After three weeks of confinement in the White House, and two weeks before her trip to the Middle East, Hernandez decided she would travel to Tucson for a brief weekend visit with her family. The evening before her scheduled departure, however, the secret service director asked to see her about an urgent matter.

"Madam President, we have received credible information indicating that your safety may be in danger if you travel to Arizona." Maybe assuming this would be enough to discourage her, he left it at that.

"I will need every scrap of detail you have on this threat before I decide how to proceed." Taken aback, the director said he would need to confer with his staff to get that information. To which Hernandez responded: "If there are people who know more about this than you do, please have them come in person to brief me."

Two persons duly reported to the president that social media monitors had spotted several badly coded posts referring to a not so secret militia band training in western New Mexico, some members of which apparently traveled to Tucson recently for unknown reasons. The band was known for its virulent anti-immigrant creed.

In one incident they had stopped a van on US 54, believing it was carrying undocumented Mexicans.   Three of their Suburbans boxed the van in on the shoulder and a posse of vigilantes approached with high-powered rifles. The occupants of the van refused to open the door and a passenger used his cell phone to call for help.

As the militia members shouted and brandished their weapons a trio of New Mexico highway patrol vehicles appeared and closed on the scene at high speed. Three of the vigilantes dropped to a knee and leveled their weapons at the oncoming officers, who stopped about twenty yards short, ordering through onboard loudspeakers for the men to drop their weapons and lie face down on the ground. One of them shouted "We are ready to die defending our homes, so do what you can!" The situation then resolved when other members talked their brothers into standing down.

The president listened to this report without expression and without comment. Then she nodded as if to say "and ...?"

"That's what we have so far, Madam President."

Her impatience barely disguised: "Nothing about any specific threat to me or my family?"

"No ma'am, except to the extent that groups like this have been quite vocal in expressing hatred for immigrants they believe are taking control of the country. And the fact of some activity in Tucson."

Hernandez stared at the men for several tense moments, trying to get a grip on conflicting emotions that simultaneously would summarily dismiss them as purveying nonsense and convey gratitude for their concern. Once her agitation settled, she told them that while she appreciated their efforts there really was no information of immediate consequence that could justify any change in plans.

However, she added, if word spread that federal law enforcement had identified this threat the "cowardly fools" may desist from endangering Hispanic people in the region. She said that she was prepared to speak about it herself if necessary.

Then, in her one public comment while in Tucson, Hernandez said that some federal law enforcement people had cautioned her about coming to Arizona, that some amateur militants may try to harm her or her family. "I came anyway. I am the Commander in Chief of our armed forces. Let such persons be warned: Neither I nor anyone in the government of the United States will be intimidated by cowardly fools who would frighten the peaceful and hard-working people of this state and this country."

It was a breathtaking pronouncement. Over the following days the president's approval rating skyrocketed.

But Adrianna Hernandez' personal well-being declined dramatically. The private toll of such public bravura was staggering. She worried mostly about her family, about her husband and her children, who must bear the brunt of her bravado. When alone with them she could not restrain her emotions and burst into crying fits.

Having grown into teenagers as children of an assertive, fearless mother, however, her son and daughter shared her spirit. They comforted her by shrugging off any danger to them and declaring that they were proud to share the perils of the presidency with her. Her husband, on the other hand, although equally supportive, could not quite hide his anxiety. Indeed, Hernandez acknowledged to him, he would hardly be human otherwise.

No incidents occurred in Arizona while the president was there.

Back at the White House she finally began to feel comfortable in the job. She slept well. Eagerness to launch the day's agenda replaced morning anxiety. The staff sensed it and rejoiced. The people responded with ever more praise and expressions of gratitude.

One morning four days before the Middle East trip she sat at breakfast scanning some newspapers and contemplating the day's agenda: visits by a delegation of Latin American manufacturing executives and the 10-year-old winners of an American history essay contest, meetings with the Joint Chiefs of Staff, the Vatican ambassador, and her economic advisers, and a live interview with CBS News. An "urgent" call came in from her communications director.

"Madam President," he said, excited but controlled, "they say you have no enemies, but a president always has at least one somewhere in the battalions of the press." Hernandez ate a spoonful of oatmeal and waited.

"Yours has surfaced with an outrageous story he swears is true. As ridiculous as it is, however, we will need to squash it immediately before its legs get active."

Another spoonful. Some coffee. "Go on."

"Well, the story is this: It seems this guy tried to find birth records for you in Tucson, but was not successful. So he has been digging in the Mexican mud. Talking to people in your mother's hometown – Cananea isn't it?"

"Yes, that's right. My father also came from Cananea."

"Apparently, our heroic journalist found some old lady who said she was very proud of you. When he asked her why she told him she had known your mother and that she remembers the day you were born, that she even held you for a few minutes."

Swallowing coffee too fast. Burning the back of her throat. "How is that possible?"

"Yeah I know. Fanciful memory. The guy asked if that was in Tucson. She said no, never been there. It was right there in Cananea. She said she remembers because your mother left a few days later to join her husband in America."

A strange shudder made her put down the toast she was about to eat. She did not feel threatened by the story, but she knew it was going to cause trouble she did not want or need.

"Anyway, with your permission, I will arrange for the birth records to be located, copied, and sent to me in case we need them. In the meantime, do you think your mother would be able to make a statement?"

The trouble already has started. Her mother was not well. She did not need this either. "I will see what I can do," she said quietly. "What is the status of the story?"

"His organization has asked us for comment. They plan to put it out tomorrow."

"Let me know when you have the records."

To relieve the anxiety that had returned in full force Hernandez decided not to wait before checking with her mother. She called. Her brother answered. "How is Mama?"

"Not too good," he said. "She is very distraught. Crying all the time."

"What about?"

"Oh I thought you knew all about it. And that's why you're calling. Reporters showed up here last night. Wanted to talk to her. Papa called me and I came. I talked to them.

"'Why you want to bother my mother?' I said. 'Just want to ask her a question' they said. 'What question?' I said. 'You can ask me.' 'Ok,' they said. 'Is it true that your sister Adrianna was born in Cananea, Mexico, not here in Tucson?' I said 'No, that's ridiculous. Somebody is making up stories.'

"Then they said that a woman named Carmen Rodriguez in Cananea had said so. I told them she was either senile or lying and I would like to know how much she was paid. 'The story is false,' I said and would not let them talk to Mama. By that time some of our friends were here and threatened trouble if they didn't leave. So they left.

"But when I told Mama what they said she freaked out and started bawling like somebody died. Papa too looked like in shock or something. I said what's going on? And finally when he got the nerve, he looked at me and said 'The story is true. Adrianna was born in Cananea. In Mexico.'"

PART II

It is August 4, 1787. A lawyer wakes up early in his Philadelphia home, but lies in bed contemplating the day ahead. His practice flourishing, on most Saturdays he will spend the morning hours working in his office attached to the house. There are a number of matters waiting for his attention: land title disputes, surveying contract litigation, trust disbursement negotiations, defense of a criminal trespass charge. After dinner and a brief nap, he and his wife normally will ride their carriage around the town to visit friends. Later they will receive visitors, some of whom will stay for a light supper in the evening.

Today, however, will be different. Today he has a task before him that will consume every hour from when he gets himself downstairs and into his chair until some ridiculously late time of the night.

There is a deadline. Not for him specifically, at least it was not originally. It is the deadline imposed on the committee of which he is only one of five distinguished members. Yet, as of about dusk yesterday, when a messenger from the committee chair arrived with a package of his and the other members' fragmentary notes and the message that a printer had been alerted to receive the draft tomorrow morning, the emergency became his problem.

It is a problem only because he has so little time. He has no doubt about his ability to complete the project. A brilliant lawyer, he is renowned for his intellect among knowledgeable men throughout the embryonic nation. And he inherited a vigorous capacity for getting things done from his parents and ancestors, who farmed the tough soil spread across the hills of Fife, a Scottish peninsula bounded by the North Sea, the Firth of

Tay, and the Firth of Forth. Everything he has gained came from his own effort. Unlike other men leading the convention proceeding that summer in Philadelphia, his accomplishments never rested on the backs of other human beings bought and sold as slaves.

His family was poor, but determined that the oldest son would receive the education required to become a minister. He entered the University of St. Andrews, seven miles from his hometown of Ceres. There he was immersed in the new ideas and modes of thought produced by Scottish Enlightenment scholars. However, he did not enter the ministry.

Instead he came to America, in 1765, when he was twenty-three. He did not have money. He did not own property. He had only a few letters of introduction and fierce determination.

He had to work very hard to survive. An exceptional knowledge of Latin enabled him to tutor the subject at the College of Philadelphia. Now eyeing a career in law, he apprenticed in a prominent law office. After a year of intensive and meticulous study, he was eligible to practice on his own. He opened a practice in the frontier town of Reading, 65 miles northwest of Philadelphia.

With peerless energy, knowledge, and analytical skills, he became a master of the property litigation that dominated the legal world of Bucks County. Financial success and professional renown followed. As did a vital role in the political ferment stirring in the colonies in response to England's oppressive policies.

A pamphlet he wrote but did not publish until 1774 established him as one of the first to question the authority of Parliament to legislate for the colonies. When finally published, the pamphlet drew immediate acclaim from the intellectual elite of every colony. It also elevated him to widespread prominence.

He moved back to Philadelphia, the epicenter of

revolutionary debate and was appointed to represent Pennsylvania at the Continental Congress. Once the colony rescinded its instructions to oppose independence, he became an active supporter and signed the Declaration of Independence.

The ensuing years were productive and perilous. The work he did during this time prepared him above all his colleagues for the task they are facing this summer. He helped to create a state bank to fund the American army. After the state Assembly scuttled that bank, he defended the Bank of North America, charted by Congress and Pennsylvania, through years of attack by radicals seeking to revoke the state charter.

Exhibiting extraordinary personal bravery, he successfully defended 19 of 23 defendants accused of treason in the midst of war-time hysteria. This, along with misperceptions about his role in declaring independence, inflamed a mob that assaulted his house. He and some friends barricaded inside were compelled to fire on the mob and six people were killed before city troops intervened.

When a group of American sailors captured a British ship on which they had been prisoners a Pennsylvania admiralty court awarded them only a fraction of the prize money. Arguing for the sailors on appeal to the commissioners assigned by the Continental Congress to decide prize matters, he obtained reversal of the order. However, the Pennsylvania court refused to obey the commissioners' decision, thus demonstrating a critical weakness in the political organization set up under the Articles of Confederation and the necessity of establishing national judicial power.

By 1786 that political organization had broken down to the point that a meeting to discuss solutions had ended with a call for the states to send representatives to Philadelphia the next summer for a convention that would debate revisions to the Articles. He was among those chosen to attend.

Now, almost two months after the convention began, he is expected to prepare a draft constitution embodying the twenty-three general resolutions agreed to by the convention. He is one member of the Committee of Detail assigned the job -- to be completed while the rest of the delegates enjoy a ten-day recess. As one of the most predominant voices debating the resolutions his selection to the committee seemed inevitable.

Any expectations he had for a truly collaborative process, however, were dispelled within a few days, after the other members excused themselves from joint personal deliberations and offered only piecemeal comments and suggestions instead. Yesterday the chairman made a significant effort to sketch a rudimentary framework, but even his contribution did not produce anything close to a complete draft. Now only one day remains. And it is entirely up to him.

The resolutions themselves hardly constitute a constitution. They really are no more than a conceptual outline, a synopsis of those fundamental features a majority of men with acutely diverse agendas could accept. If he cannot write them into a functional plan, by adding what he believes are essential practical details, the committee will fail, the convention will fail, and most likely the new nation will fail.

One notion steadies him as he finally rises and dresses and makes his way downstairs, his middle-aged bones reacting to each step down the hardwood staircase: This will not be the last word. He need not worry that what he does today will end up chiseled in stone for decades to come. The future of the nation will not depend on the words he scratches out this day. Because one feature he certainly will include is a process for amending the constitution or revising it or rewriting it altogether as its components prove defective or impractical or unwise as the country grows. So he and his convention colleagues need not contemplate too far into posterity; they must produce a blueprint adequate to the founding of a stable government, but perfection of the plan will be subject to future deliberations.

He is comforted and moved also by the enormity of the role he is about to play in this momentous act. If he succeeds, and the document is adopted, and the nation thrives upon it and its subsequent editions, his fame will live down the ages. The prospect leaves him almost breathless when he enters the office, bolts the door shut, lowers his anxious body into the cracking leather chair that has held him all these years, and spreads the papers before him across the desk.

After cleaning his well-worn spectacles with a cotton cloth he keeps nearby for the purpose, and dipping a quill in the refilled ink jar, he flattens a blank paper and begins to write words that have been appearing in his mind for several weeks. It is a preamble. And his choice of the introductory phrase reflects what to him is the bedrock foundation of the new nation and the charter he is preparing: "We the People ..."

Because from the commencement of the convention he has been at odds with most of the other delegates about the true source of their authority and the authority that will be vested in the new government. He has vociferously advocated for a legislative branch constituted by proportional representation, so that it fairly represents the people. Acknowledging that its adoption was not likely, he nevertheless has proposed and repeatedly advocated that the person serving as head of the executive be elected directly by the people.

But the other delegates, like most of their fellow American aristocrats, are afraid of the people. They agree only to institutions or officers selected by other institutions: A senate selected by members of the other house or by the state legislatures. A chief executive selected by the senate.

Compromises were not avoidable. So the constitution he will draft provides for one legislative house that is proportional to population and another that is not. It also will set forth a scheme to elect a chief executive that is the closest he could get to a true voice of the people: Electors from each state who will cast votes for the candidate who prevailed in that state, the number of electors for each state to be nearly proportional to population. Neither the national nor the state legislatures will have hands in the process.

The draft also will include many provisions that the convention has not even discussed, much less approved. Some of these were suggested and agreed to by the other members of the committee. However, most of them are coming from his own mind, terms that he believes are essential for the constitution to be effective and the nation durable.

Thus he adds a list of powers that will be granted to the two legislative houses and another list of powers the individual states may not exercise. He adds a clause empowering the national legislature to make all laws that are necessary and proper for executing the powers granted to the national government. Whereas the convention has resolved that the acts of the national legislature will be supreme, he broadens this provision significantly to declare that the constitution itself, along with the legislative acts, shall be "the supreme law of the several states", the judges of the states to "be bound thereby in their decisions".

The convention has adopted resolutions to establish a national judiciary, but they contain few specifics about jurisdiction. He adds many missing details. He adds the clauses on privileges and immunities and full faith and credit and detailed refinements of the chief executive's powers.

Given his singular, brilliant, and heroic accomplishment this day, and his many other contributions to creation and ratification of the constitution, the name James Wilson should be honored in his time and celebrated in posterity as much or more than those of other founders. However, instead he will know only humiliation, and his name will be erased from the nation's memory.

Rightfully expecting to be named the first Chief Justice of the Supreme Court, he will be named merely an associate justice. His long struggle to achieve a financial position equal to the land-wealthy, slave-holding American aristocrats eventually will pull him into massive debt.   He will be thrown in debtor's prison. He will flee the state to avoid creditors and die alone on August 21, 1798, holed up in a room over a tavern in Edentown, North Carolina.

The chief author of the constitution, one of its greatest champions, the founder most instrumental to the phenomenal outcome of the convention and the birth and robust life of a great nation, Wilson's destiny is to be utterly forgotten. Through the coming decades and centuries historians, biographers, scholars, and journalists will write countless works about his convention colleagues and fellow founders. And virtually nothing about him.

The slave masters will be honored most of all. There will be great monuments dedicated to them. Children will learn about them as inseparable from the nation's beginnings and its ultimate greatness. Their names will be recognized throughout the world, synonymous with freedom and liberty, their profound hypocrisy ignored.

No one -- no historian, no biographer, no scholar or journalist of any kind -- will write even a paragraph about this man for almost 200 years. And even then, the light shown on him and his contribution will be like a candle flame burning in blazing sunlight.

The fundamental principle Wilson tries to embody in the constitution will remain inchoate, a celebrated abstraction, until actuated more than seven decades later after civil war. Ghosts of the sacred slave masters will support a confederate rebellion to preserve their human property. But the People will defeat the rebellion. And Abraham Lincoln will articulate Wilson's principle again when he describes in his Gettysburg Address a "government of the people, by the people, for the people"

PART III

On a carved wood pedestal in the corner of the room is a three-foot-tall Japanese bronze sculpture from the late 19th century, an elephant, tusks uplifted, fighting off attacking lions. Adjacent to it, across the end wall, is a six-panel mixed media piece of collaged paper, ink, and paint on an iridescent surface. The artist: Paul Horiuchi, renowned Northwest Artist of layered expressionism known for the elegance of his work, which is valued at six figures a piece.

Surrounding a massive smooth mahogany conference table and arranged against opposite walls are 26 very dark brown full-grain leather chairs. Those fortunate enough to take outside facing seats gaze over a spectacular panorama of the San Francisco Bay only viewable from the 31st floor corner conference room of Carlisle & Crum, according to its website the most distinguished law firm in the city.

Entering the room and pouring water into crystal cups from crystal pitchers, one swaggering lawyer after another greets the host, silver-haired, bushy-eyebrowed, baritone-voiced Roger Crum, who, though seventy-six and barely ambulatory, stands behind his chair at the head of the table until thirty four burnished bodies in elegant suits have settled into place either in the luxurious chairs or standing between them against a wall.

Before carefully lowering himself into a seat, Mr. Crum announces that everyone is invited to lunch at Le Grande Dapur. The Rendang there is superb, he notes. "And after our chores are done for the day, we will assemble at The Fontaigne to enjoy a few bottles of Chateau Montelena Napa Chardonnay, 2009 I believe."

Besides Roger Crum, his partners Paul Figerau and Helen Wainwright are also present. While Mr. Crum likes to boast that his hourly rate has remained $550 for ten years, Mr. Figerau and

Ms. Wainwright last year increased theirs from $650 to $675 and $575 to $625, respectively.

Among others attending the meeting are Jack Melhuse and Richard Krane from the New York firm of Mostov, Melhuse, Price & Krane. Mr. Melhuse also charges $675 for each hour he spends talking about the matter, Mr. Krane only $575. They had adjacent seats in the first-class cabin flying out, so naturally they talked about the matter throughout.

Katherine Stamp and Ed Wingate are there from Chicago. They graciously accept congratulations on their big win before the Seventh Circuit in the Parslow Mining case, which affirmed the validity of land sale contracts Parslow had made with several destitute property owners. The company considers protection by the contract clause of the US Constitution well worth the $16.75 million legal fee.

"Shall we get down to business," Mr. Crum says. "Everyone knows the situation, so we don't need to delve too deep into the details. But I thought to begin I would have my partner, Paul Figerau, briefly frame the issue. Paul."

"Thanks Roger. Before I begin, I just want to say a few words about how extraordinary this effort is. The best legal minds around all concentrating on a single question of immense gravity. I hope everyone is cognizant of the place in history assumed by this group..." And more of the same for fifteen minutes, until "and so, with that, let me begin the discussion with this query: The Constitution, Article II, Section1: No person except a natural born citizen, or a citizen of the United States, at the time of the adoption of this Constitution, shall be eligible to the office of President. What does this mean?"

He scans the faces, intense, solemn. "What does this language mean?" No one can return his stare. Each looks down at the crystal glass they caress nervously or, if they can, gaze out across the bay, anything to avoid having Paul Figerau think they know the answer. Then he concludes with grand significance and drama, "That is our task," and sits down.

"Thanks Paul," Mr. Crum says, nodding his head filled with the weight of history. "Now many of you know that we are not writing on a completely empty canvass. There are a few precedents. None that are very helpful, however. I asked Helen Wainwright if she could briefly review what we have. Helen."

"Thank you, Roger. Hello everyone. First, I want to echo Paul's words about the moment we are experiencing. Roger is correct. These issues have been addressed, but only somewhat tangentially, so we are looking, really, from a fresh place. The most recent cases involving challenges to the eligibility of particular candidates have resulted in dismissal on standing grounds. They will not help us. So we need to go back to the earlier opinions that tackled the question, in different contexts, of what the term 'natural born citizen' means. The most often mentioned in the literature is the Supreme Court's opinion in United States v. Wong Kim Ark from 1898. Justice Gray's lengthy discussion plowed through English common law precedents looking at the term in the contexts of inheritance and the like, and focusing on the concept of allegiance, that is, the status of a person at birth vis a vis the power of government and the person's duties of obedience. However, the issue in Wong Kim Ark was whether the Chinese exclusion act applied to a person born in the United States to parents living here but who remained subject to the Chinese emperor. Again, not really a helpful circumstance. Of similar effect are a series of district court decisions from the early 1900s. The first of these was –"

Mr. Crum interrupts with "Helen, have you prepared any written material?"

"Well, I have a number of associates working on it. We do not have the finished memorandum yet." This seems to satisfy the old gentleman. "Anyway, so we have these lower court decisions..."

The discussion dribbles on in the same vein for another 90 minutes before Crum wakes up surprised that the Rendang has not been served. Realizing that the meeting is still in progress, he ends it and again invites everyone to lunch at Le Grande Dapur. It will be a working lunch, he says. The meters will keep running.

2

For a full ten days President Hernandez has held on to her office, merely allowing aides to issue cryptic statements concerning her and her lawyers' need to study the matters raised by the new information about her birthplace. She was ready to resign, if that was the only option. But she was not going to let the People's will be thwarted without careful consideration.

These public postures screened a massive effort to save the President. Many millions of dollars have enriched ten law firms and more than 55 lawyers and professors. Thousands more have gone for the gastronomic delicacies and sumptuous accommodations legal minds require for superior thinking and for access to the electronic vault where all legal information generated by humanity is kept.

Legions of experts in law have scoured the sources, turned every rock, shined the light of research into every obscure recess, every nook, every cranny, every hitherto neglected corner. They have produced massive memos, packed with details of each step taken, each theory tested, each event explained and analyzed, every statement, query, quip, aside, comment, declaration, request, indeed every word no matter how trivial, ever uttered and recorded by anyone remotely entitled to be classed as a founder. They have digested thousands of pounds of scholarship. And what has this extraordinary, unprecedented, colossal campaign of legal investigation, research, and analysis found as grounds that made Adrianna Hernandez eligible to be president despite having entered the world in Mexico? Nothing.

They found a single scrap of legislative history: A letter John Jay, who was not a delegate to the 1787 constitutional convention, sent to George Washington on July 25, 1787:

> "Permit me to hint, whether it would be wise and seasonable to provide a strong check to the admission of Foreigners into the administration of our national Government; and to declare expressly that the Commander in Chief of the American army shall not be given to nor devolve on, any but a natural born Citizen."

Apparently, Washington took the *hint* and the clause was inserted.

Yet even as legislative history the letter is virtually worthless. Not only does it throw no light on the meaning or intent of the clause; it does not qualify as an expression by any of the constitution's actual framers. Consequently, since there was no discussion of the clause recorded or mentioned anywhere, the legal battalions have no legislative history to work with.

All they can present, for lack of a more elegant expression, is bullshit. Vacuous homilies about the significance of custom and tradition and democracy, about progress and change and technicalities pointless in the modern world, about leadership and inspiring leaders and the irrelevance of a great leader's origins. Twenty-two pages analyzing the syntax of the eligibility clause. Another nineteen comparing and contrasting the clause with other Constitutional phrases.   Speculation disguised as assurances that the creators of the Constitution did not and could not have intended for the clause to be used in these circumstances. A most erudite examination and recitation of the use by English courts over the centuries of the term "natural born" and the concept of being a "natural born citizen", transformed through superb sophistry into an argument favoring Hernandez's right to be president.

Of course, there are other sides contending to the contrary. Although, believing the plain language of the clause is unequivocal and not susceptible to any meaning different from what it clearly says, they have not employed similar legal legions to make the case. In general they argue that the Supreme Court can and should declare that Hernandez is not eligible to be president. What happens then they are not able to say. Presumably, Hernandez, being the very ethical and moral being that she is, will acknowledge the declaration and resign. But what if she doesn't?

The persons demanding Hernandez' resignation, voluntary or otherwise, include some vocal members of congress, constitutional law professors, all but one of the living former presidents, and the one person who might actually have standing to pursue a legal case: Vice-President Mike Jordan. He can hardly contain his eagerness to get Hernandez out so that he can assume the office he has sought for so long. Shrugging off aspersions on his loyalty, Jordan rationalizes his actions as beneficial to the country and actually to Hernandez. She is not comfortable in the job, he implies, so he will come to her rescue by taking over. Hernandez herself has been stone silent on Jordan's betrayal.

PART IV

His foot was still sore from kicking the copy machine at tray number four when the error message insisted that sector was to blame for the jam that stopped production of the trial exhibits. Kat, his assistant, was still at the copy service waiting for at least the first set. That way he could tell the judge in the morning that he was ready to proceed. Even if the client did not show up for their preparation meeting, which seemed likely now that it was 5:30 and he had expected her at 4:00. The subpoena had been served on her ex-husband, so all that could be done to bring in the main witness was done, and the judge could not dismiss the case despite his repeated threats.

He did need to plug some citations into the trial brief, sometime before Kat printed it, sometime before tomorrow morning, hopefully no later than eight. If he could find any. It did not seem like that arcane of a partnership issue. Wife marries husband and joins his chiropractic practice. Husband burns out, frightens the patients with violent hand gestures, calls them lazy spineless worms, drives them away, defaults on the lease the wife never signed, and, after the divorce, lets the insurance carrier for the partnership settle with the two patients who sue. Carrier then sues husband and wife for indemnity. Wife hires lawyer referred to her by divorce attorney, who rents space in the same office building. Lawyer files cross-action against husband, which is the only claim left after the carriers' suit is settled.

The lawyer is Frank Wayne. Wayne does business as The Law Offices of Frank Wayne and Associates. But there are no associates. Just Frank Wayne. And Kat Moreno, his assistant, secretary, office manager, bookkeeper.

Wayne's office is at the corner of Light and East

Montgomery streets in Baltimore. It is a small office, two rooms and a bathroom. Kat works in one room at a gray metal desk, surrounded by stacks of boxes, many crumpling under pressure from those piled on them, the bottom ones grimy with dark green film. There are boxes in Wayne's room too, and piles of paper resting on the beige polyester carpet, two straight-backed guest chairs with wicker trim, and his eight-foot dark walnut desk that he sits behind in a rust leather executive chair covered with silver blotches that might be errant shots of spray paint. Wayne has a Dell laptop computer that he is struggling to keep working now two years past its life expectancy.

Kat returned pulling a luggage carrier and a box of exhibits. She asked if the brief was ready to print, knowing full well that it was not, and whether he had anything else for her, quickly adding "if not I'll be off" before he could respond. She left him to search his online Westlaw service for helpful authority. The client did not appear and did not call.

Someone did call. Opposing counsel in another case. Wayne answered because he thought it was the client. Instant regret.

"I want to resume the deposition next Tuesday," he said. "Do I need to go in ex parte?"

Wayne did not even look at the calendar before replying: "I guess so if you insist on Tuesday. I just can't do it then. Got trial starting tomorrow and –"

"That's bullshit. You expect me to sit on my hands and wait while the rascal Frank Wayne tries to clear up his calendar? Ain't gonna happen. It was bullshit when you stopped the deposition, bullshit every time you put it off again, and bullshit now. Tired of it."

"So go in for your ex parte."

"Tired of your attitude too. Your god damned slimy, evasive attitude. A little cooperation now and then would –"

"Mr. Snedicker I've got things to do. Trial tomorrow. Other things. If you're just going to yell at me I will have to cut this off."

"Jesus! We all got things to do." Then, in a low weary tone, "You'll get the notice." He hung up.

The exchange left Wayne anxious and depressed. He felt like he was shaking, but he was not. Half an hour or so went by before he even tried once again to concentrate on the trial brief.

Frank Wayne did not believe that he was slimy or evasive or uncooperative. He was just a regular civil litigation lawyer struggling to pull in enough fees to pay rent for his office and his studio apartment, his staff, his liability insurance premiums that kept rising, the monthly on his ten-year-old Toyota Camry that he had refinanced three years ago, and the rest of the expenses his simple and dreary life required. He no longer paid a mortgage. No more alimony as of last year when his ex remarried. He kicked in some support for their two teenagers when he could spare it, but she had given up trying to collect it. After fifteen years he was still in practice, still working solo, still getting new matters every few months, still winning, losing, and settling at the same rate.

Lately, however, for about the past six or seven months, he had begun to sense a growing bitterness, nothing acute, nothing, he was sure, anyone else would notice, expressed so far in a tendency to see mean motives in people, to consider routine requests by other lawyers and judges and even clients as actuated by a desire to make him feel ridiculous. The first time he realized the subtle change was when he started to receive emails from law school acquaintances hoping to arrange a party the day before their formal twentieth reunion. There was nothing in the messages he could identify as the cause. They were quite friendly and said nothing about what anyone was doing, no boasts about so and so becoming such and such federal judge. Maybe it was the fact that he had no wish to respond, had no wish to see any of them, and, in fact, hated the very idea.

Actually Wayne went to his law school ten-year reunion. That was ten years ago, five years after he left the Department of Justice's Constitutional and Specialized Tort Litigation Section, where he went to work after finishing at the University of Baltimore Law School. Somehow – he long ago suppressed details of the feat – he managed to complete the first year at Georgetown and was desperately groping towards another semester when his will gave out. He left the program abruptly, went to his mother's home in Hagerstown and hid from the University of Maryland friends who called to find out what happened. His mother indulged him for three weeks, then delivered an ultimatum: get a job or get back in school. He transferred to the University of Baltimore and started there in January.

For a year or so the work at Justice was very stimulating. He helped to defend a customs agent who was sued by a blind Sikh after the agent detained him for an hour to determine why a powerful odor something like sulfur was coming from his crotch. Once the agent found the rotten onions in the Sikh's underwear he was released, but not before the community pick-up service concluded that he had not arrived and left the airport. The Sikh was forced to take a cab, but on route disclosed to the driver that he had no money and was deposited by the side of a congested turnpike where he was struck and injured by a passenger van trying to pass traffic on the shoulder.

But already two years into the job Wayne was burning out. It wasn't the legal work. It was more the social work, the political work, the work of having to report up the line, to justify what he did, of having to write memoranda explaining his conclusions and strategies and recommendations, and then so often having to suffer through personal conferences where his supervisor and her supervisors and some of his colleagues droned through hours of wasted time discussing what to him were trivial details the summer interns could scrutinize, that did not require an assembly of department big heads.

When he had repaid all but $5,000 of his student loans he left and set off on his own. Using a gift or loan – it was never clear which – from his mother he leased the office he still used fifteen years later. The announcement cards he sent out to every person he had ever met who might remember him paid some benefit after a couple of months. Phone contacts here and there led to a few small matters which led to a few more and by the first-year anniversary he was collecting enough to pay rent and the insurance premiums.

Wild fluctuations in regular revenue troubled his practice from then on, but he never went under enough to think about giving up. And there was the occasional successful contingency case.

The reunion was more fun than he had expected. Probably because of the martinis. And the shared recall of events and persons that were still fresh.

Like the day professor Fitzhugh collapsed while describing the "beauty" of a particular subtitle from the Internal Revenue Code. A former paramedic in the class performed CPR and kept him breathing until the EMTs arrived and took him away. Wayne thought it strange that no one at the reunion knew what had ever happened to the professor.

Like when the two fattest women there sat naked through three classes in protest of the dean's suggestion that female lawyers should be more conscious of how their appearance affects judges and juries. Those at the reunion who discussed the event generally agreed that the awkward tension muffled everyone's intellect and demonstrated at least that the art of advocacy was much more multifaceted than they thought.

Wayne's favorite reminiscence had been the tale of Patrick

Marius, an adjunct associate professor of legal history. Everyone who had taken his course remembered vividly his obsession with James Wilson, who Marius insisted was the real father of the United States Constitution.

Wayne remember one oft-repeated rant triggered by some mention of James Madison: "Ah yes," Marius would begin, "the so-called father of the thing. The same guy who came up with the three-fifths compromise crap. The guy who inscribed the nation's acceptance of slavery into the wet concrete of the foundation so that a huge portion of the people would forever have only three-fifths the value of the rest. The guy who himself owned more than 100 slaves and never freed them. This is our honored founder. This is bullshit!"

Wayne also recalled that Marius many times during the term announced that he intended to found a campaign for re-writing the constitution. To clean it up, he explained. To delete from the official body of the document all the provisions that had been amended out of it. He said he never understood why the official version still contained all the original language, much of it patently racist, that was modified only by a subsequent amendment that a reader must proceed many paragraphs, almost a hundred years, and through a horrible civil war to see. We need to create a new constitution, he said, not necessarily new substantively, not necessarily one that would affect the actual law derived from it, but that would affect the way it was cited or referred to, so that instead of citing an "amendment" we would cite to the original. Like is the case for every other law in the land.

Another episode Wayne recalled was when Marius suddenly stopped lecturing and looked intently around the classroom as if searching for the right victim. Once he had selected someone he asked the student: "Can you identify the real father of the constitution, the man who single handedly actually created the bulk of it?" The student nervously responded, "Not

James Madison?" Marius smiled patronizingly and said "no, not the slave master."

Then he asked the class at large: "Does anyone know who it was that spoke as often at the convention as the slave master, offered as many or more ideas than the slave master, and who actually hand wrote the original constitution, adding on his own accord major substantive provisions that passed virtually unchanged into the official product and through the history of the nation?" Blank faces all around.

"Be aware that I am not surprised in the least that none of you know. Almost no one does. Even so-called scholars of the subject. How many books have been written about the slave master and his fellow slave masters George Washington, Thomas Jefferson, and James Monroe? Hundreds. How many books have been written about James Wilson? None." Then shouting, face coloring pale orange, eyes swelling open: "None! One skimpy biography in the '50s. That's it. How can that be?"

One afternoon Wayne passed Marius walking absorbed in some trouble of the mind and whispering to it. He did not seem to notice Wayne. But as Wayne went on a few paces he heard: "Hey, you're in my class." He turned and saw Marius in a different context, sunlight instead of florescent. Thin, sharply angular face. Light brown hair brushed straight back. Scraggly goatee. Green plaid sweater with threads hanging at the elbows.

He was in one of his depressive moods. He asked Wayne if anyone in the class had been upset by his tirade. He apologized to Wayne, even though Wayne said it was not necessary and that actually the episode had sparked up an otherwise very boring day. Marius seemed a little offended by this, but shrugged it off and explained that a captive audience was the only kind that ever listened. But he knew that trouble was coming if he did not simmer down.

At the reunion Wayne learned that soon after trouble had

indeed come. Marius taught the legal history course over three terms, but then the university did not renew his contract. A university representative responded to his inquiry for the reason by saying that it was an issue of competence.

Marius threatened to sue the university if they did not provide more information. Thus pressed, and to avoid further trouble, the university sent Marius a confidential letter explaining that events which had occurred during his last term had caused unidentified faculty administrators to question his mental competence.

After an investigation that included interviews of several students, the university concluded that Marius was mentally unstable, possibly suffering from paranoid schizophrenia, and prone to acting out in a manner that could be harmful to his students and colleagues. The university suggested that he seek mental health treatment and offered to consider him again for a position once he had done so and if appropriately certified by a psychiatrist.

About three years after the reunion Wayne was startled one day by the story linked to a small headline on the Baltimore Sun's website: "LOCAL MAN ARRESTED AFTER HOSTAGE DRAMA IN PHILADELPHIA".

> A man who was arrested in Philadelphia Thursday after briefly holding hostage an employee of the Historical Society of Pennsylvania is a former resident of Towson and taught at several local schools.
>
> The man, identified as Patrick Marius, allegedly entered the Society's building on Locust Street, told the receptionist he was a professor of legal history, and wanted to do some research in the

papers of James Wilson. Apparently, Marius was guided to the appropriate collections area, where he filled out a request form. Some minutes later a member of the library staff brought Marius a box containing an assortment of Wilson papers.

The unidentified staff member reported later that Marius became upset when he found only photostats of the documents he wanted in the box. The staff member tried to explain that the originals are secured in a vault only accessible by authorized employees and members of the public who sign up for a special "Behind the Scenes" tour that costs $500.

Marius allegedly then grabbed the woman, put her into a headlock, and held a sharp pencil to her neck, demanding that she take him to the vault. Almost immediately someone called the police and two officers who were nearby responded. They confronted Marius, ordered him to release the woman and lie on the floor. When he refused they approached him with a taser. He backed away, pulling the woman with him and threatening to jab the pencil into her neck.

The officers then tried to talk Marius out of the situation. But more police arrived, and he became even more agitated. He began to shout: "I need to see those documents! I don't want to hurt the lady, but I will do what I must to see those documents."

The officers explained that the only document

COMMITTEE OF DETAIL   90

Marius was likely to see was a criminal indictment. By this time one of the new officers had managed to get behind Marius while he was distracted with his speech. The officer deftly pulled Marius' arm away from the woman's neck and wrestled him to the floor. Marius began whimpering and saying "I'm sorry" repeatedly. He did not resist as he was cuffed and led out of the building.

Although he intended to find out if and where Marius was being held, and to follow the story from there, Wayne did not follow up. Marius obviously had not cured his mental issues. His James Wilson obsession still gripped his mind. Maybe this event will have positive results for him. Maybe he will get some kind of probation with an order for psychotherapy. Yes, of course. The thought calmed the strange anxiety Wayne felt. There was nothing for him to do about Marius. He would be taken care of.

Wayne enjoyed the reunion also because then he still relished the feel of singularity, of being a maverick, if not exactly an outlaw. Where his acquaintances told of all night marathons finishing section IX. B.1.a. of an important brief for the Fourth Circuit he countered with the tale of the bar owner he defended from an unlawful detainer suit alleging the bar was the home base for a certain group of bookies. One alum who heard the story remembered it and referred the owner of a strip club to him for a similar case.

Actually that type of small business person had increasingly become his typical client. For some reason he could not settle on, over the past three or four years a number of persons in what was customarily categorized as "the adult entertainment business" had contacted him to represent them in various small matters usually involving less than $10,000.

Just that afternoon Kat had taken a message from someone

who had leased a vacant retail space where he was opening some kind of private club. He did not say what kind. The place was just about ready to open when suddenly a small group of demonstrators had appeared outside apparently bent on preventing patrons from entering or at least to harass them on their way in. Call Frank Wayne, a former business associate told him.

He gave up trying to find good citations for the trial brief. Instead he put in some he had used before but that really had little to do with the points he tied to them. Hoping the judge would not bother or have time to check. Hoping the judge would assume opposing counsel was exaggerating as usual when she pretended to be outraged by Wayne's disregard for correctly stating the law. Thumbing through the exhibits with no enthusiasm, he wrote a note for Kat to print the brief and bring it to him at the courthouse before she went to pick up the other copies. And to call the client to see if she might actually show up for trial.

2

Wayne woke up late. Well, he didn't wake up late, but he finally willed himself out of bed half an hour past the time he should have been down in the garage starting his car. No time for coffee. No time for food. No shower. He had to just suit up and go. Fortunately, his briefcase and document bag were in the car already, where he left them the night before after grimly concluding that he was not going to look at anything they contained before he arrived at the courthouse in the morning. A pulsating ache burned up the back of his neck and into the aft section of his brain. Another hovered over his eyes. Without caffeine he would continue to suffer.

The line for coffee at the drive-through was too long for

the anxiety building in his stomach. The stuff he picked up from the deli cart outside the elevator scalded his throat when he drank it too fast trying to finish it before pushing through the heavy wooden doors into the courtroom of Judge David Goliath, who did not permit any beverage besides water.

"Mr. Wayne, the judge wants to see you and Ms. Monroe in his chambers," the clerk said as she spotted him. Andrea Monroe sat smugly at the counsel table.

"Are you ready this time, Mr. Wayne?" the judge asked without even looking up as the two lawyers appeared at the rear of his somewhat barren chambers.

"Ready, your honor," Wayne announced, blustering the nervousness from his voice.

"Fine. Do you have any papers for me?" The trial brief! He had forgotten about it. Maybe Kat was outside with it.

"My assistant has our papers, your honor. May I step out to get them from her?" Judge Goliath now raised his eyes to stare at Wayne without lifting his head, focusing skeptical contempt. He waved his hand and resumed his examination of whatever papers lay before him.

Kat indeed was in the courtroom. She too had rushed, as the tiny lines of moisture across her cheeks showed. Her lavender shirt was untucked in places, her dark brown hair in need of trimming, with silver roots visible in need of coloring, was more than normally disheveled. Without speaking, she fished papers from a bag and handed them to Wayne, who also did not speak. Until he had confirmed that it was the trial brief, then: "Any word from Lindsay?"

"No. Only thing on the machine was another message from the guy who called yesterday. His name is Rafik Kemal."

The judge scowled at the first pages of his trial brief. "Okay," the judge said, "I will look at this and we'll start at 9:30 with your first witness." Wayne noted by the judge's desk clock that it was then 9:05.

Wayne paced the hall outside the courtroom waiting for Kat to report on her desperate attempts to contact Lindsay, the client and his first, probably only, witness. The pain had mushroomed to consume his head and globules of brain matter were pulsing at his temples trying to get out. The discomfort was acute, but Frank Wayne was accustomed to it. He knew how to suffer through this kind of predicament. He was not one to panic. If Lindsay did not show up, he would plead for more time, no doubt in vain. Judge Goliath would dismiss the case and Wayne would move on to the next one, having done the best he could.

Kat. No Lindsay. Client, witness, not here your honor. Something must have happened to her. One more continuance? Goliath, it turned out, was not angry at all. He was pleased. Pleased to dismiss Frank Wayne's case. He even told Wayne to "have a nice day" after he entered the order on the record.

"I cannot believe what they are doing," an agitated Rafik Kemal stammered into the phone. "I cannot believe it. They will not listen. They cannot do that. I will sue them!"

Wayne lowered the volume on his phone. "Hold on. Calm down. What are they doing?"

"They are in front. Just standing in front. With signs. I tried to talk to them. My brother tried. They will not listen. My brother wants to drive his car on the sidewalk, to hit them, or make them get out of the way. I stopped him. You have to help us."

Wayne told Kemal to meet him at his office and then chewed down a sausage and egg biscuit along with 16 ounces of coffee while driving and listening to Lindsay's hysterical explanation shrieking from the phone set on speaker. Something about her mother and another ambulance and yet one more pointless trip to the emergency room. The judge must understand, she declared. She will sign any affidavit Wayne writes up. She has been reviewing her deposition testimony, feels more confident than ever, glad she did not take the settlement offer. Can she testify in the afternoon? Any time after two.

Rafik Kemal was Turkish, living in the US as a permanent resident. Wayne judged him to be in his late 40s, early 50s. His well-trimmed black hair showed traces of gray along the temples. He wore an expensive dark green suit, probably silk, and spoke English well but with a slight accent.

He brought photographs to the meeting in Wayne's office. They showed a group of about 12 people, all but one young, perhaps early 20s, men and women, wearing white shirts and black ties, the men dark slacks, the women dark skirts. The older man wore a dark blue suit.

Some held up poster boards with hand drawn messages:

"Be angry, and do not sin: do not let the sun go down on your wrath, NOR GIVE PLACE TO THE DEVIL. Ephesians 4:26-27"

"And the dwelling place of the wicked will come to nothing. Job 8:22"

"Let death seize them; Let them go down alive into hell, For wickedness is in their dwellings and among them. Psalm 55:15"

"We need your help, Mr. Wayne. Desperately. We have loaded our fortune into the place. Now, when we are close to opening, the shitheads outside come and stick their god damn asses in the way, trying to stop us from earning a living. We have no choice. We have people ready to take care of it. But not in a legal way. They will get hurt. You understand? I am holding my brother back. I want to try a legal way first if it is possible. But there is very little time."

"Have you tried talking to them? Do they have a –"

"Impossible! They call me the Devil and will not talk! I am not the Devil, Mr. Wayne. I am a businessman. You must do something. I will pay you whatever is required."

"Tell me something about the place. It is to be a private club, correct? What kind? What is the name of it?"

Kemal tried to control his frustration and annoyance. "What does that matter? It is our business what we do there. I will tell you the name, but I don't want to reveal anything else."

"Ok, let's start with the name."

"Hell."

"The name is 'Hell'?"

"That's right."

"Nothing before or after? Just 'Hell'?"

"That's what I said." Showing signs of hostility. Wayne stared at him placidly, waiting for him to calm down. Finally, he said "I'm sorry. This situation is making me crazy."

"And that is why the demonstrators are there? Because of the name?"

"I guess so. I don't know. They will not talk to me. Maybe they will talk to you."

An intense intuitive inclination to decline the work gripped Wayne. This was the kind of matter that brought more trouble than fees. He should tell Kemal he cannot help him and be done with it. Instead, he made the same mistake he had made so many times before: Venturing just a little deeper to see what he could do before getting out.

"Now I must tell you that it will be very difficult for me to help you without knowing what the club is all about. The court, the agencies we may have to deal with, will want to know."

Kemal drew a deep breath, apparently to settle his nerves. Then smiled. "I do not wish to inform you unless I am compelled to do so. If it is not necessary, I prefer that you not be involved to that extent."

While Kemal's smug arrogance and reticence irritated Wayne, he realized that he did not give a damn what went on inside. But if there was to be litigation about the name it surely would reach into the activities it stood for. And on its face the name did not exactly suggest wholesome fun. Convincing a judge to enjoin the demonstrators without revealing some semblance of a business plan would be difficult at best. Wayne hated to turn away work. He could not afford to. Yet he had enough integrity to refuse a responsibility he knew he could not fulfill or at least to make sure the would-be client's eyes were open when he signed the retainer agreement.

"The thing is here, Rafik, I do not believe that I can accomplish what you want, especially if I am ignorant of what it is you do. The court will certainly wish to know before it slaps an injunction on these people."

Kemal stared at Wayne, unblinking, his face turning slightly pink. "That is very unfortunate," he said slowly. "I had thought maybe the Constitution would protect us. I am extremely sad to be mistaken." For an instant Wayne thought Kemal's eyes were moistening, as if he was about to cry.

"The Constitution will protect your speech and probably your right to use the name. But as a practical matter I am not confident that I can get a judge to invoke the protection for some secret activity that, for all he knows, could be illegal and/or harmful to the public, which the name itself strongly suggests. Now it may be a somewhat different matter if there were a religious element involved. But otherwise —"

His expression suddenly brightening, Kemal interrupted: "A religious element! Yes, that's it! That's what is going on. That is what we will be doing – a religious thing."

Switching on a mask of severe skepticism, Wayne pointed out that Kemal had described Hell as a business, not a religious establishment. Furthermore, religious activity did not qualify for protection just because its sponsors labeled it religious. There were certain indicia that had to be demonstrated. And the judge would need to be convinced that the beliefs were sincerely held.

None of which seemed to dampen Kemal's enthusiasm. Demonstrating the religious aspect would not be a problem. He and his associates were deeply religious, and Hell was to be a strong component or product of their religion. After all, Hell is a place devised by religion. That is why the losers outside it are trying to prevent it from opening. The law would clear them away. He was certain that Wayne could make it happen.

3

The group harassing Kemal turned out to be from the New Life Congregation of Awakening, an independent church of about 50 members who met in the second-floor space of a two-story commercial building on Eastern Avenue in Baltimore. A hair salon called "Barbara's Beauty Boutique" occupied the ground floor.

The church's leader was a man born with the name Michael Masterson, who at the age of 48, some five years before Kemal retained Wayne, adopted the name Jedediah and founded the church with a handful of souls he had been counseling for drug abuse on behalf of the Circuit Court's Drug Court program. This much Wayne learned from a brief radio news report.

The church apparently did not have a website and the only google result for it referred to the same radio report and information. Neither the name Michael Masterson nor Jedediah produced anything associated with the group or the man. In order to pursue his strategy for Kemal, therefore, Wayne decided he would have to make personal contact, assuming that the church and its leader were not represented by legal counsel.

He did not want to enflame the situation outside Kemal's place, so he found the address for Barbara's Beauty Boutique and knocked on the upstairs door. No one home. So he went into Barbara's to ask when the upstairs neighbors typically were in.

"I never seen 'em," one of the beauty professionals said to Wayne over her shoulder while she tweaked a lady's hair.

"I think they come real early, before we open," another added. "And leave early too."

"We're closed Sundays. Maybe they're here daylight hours then."

Wayne asked if Barbara was there or if anyone knew who owned the building. Barbara was not there, and no one knew. He left his card for Barbara.

Frustrated, Wayne leaned against his car parked on Eastern and tried to plot his next move. He needed to make contact: Partly to find out what or whom he was dealing with, partly to see if there was another attorney he could communicate with, and partly to see if there was any chance of resolving the matter without legal action. After about ten minutes he decided there was nothing more he could do there and was about to get in the car when someone called to him from down the street. "Hello friend." A voice belonging to a man approaching him in slow steady strides. Wearing a blue suit.

Coming up and holding his hand out to shake Wayne's he appeared unusually calm and easy-going. "My name is Jedediah. Were you looking for me?"

His hair was very dark brown, almost black, except for streaks of gray across his temples. Thin face, high forehead, and large open ears. Slightly taller than Wayne and quite erect in posture. He spoke with pronounced even volume, as if those who wished to hear what he had to say would have to listen – he was not going to speak louder for their benefit. Nonetheless, Wayne's salient impression was of a man who exuded affability.

"Well, yes I was. Or at least somebody representing your .. group. I'm Frank Wayne, an attorney representing Rafik Kemal, the owner of the place you have been picketing. Perhaps you have a legal representative I should speak to?"

"No Mr. Wayne. Thank you for inquiring. We have no representative besides me. Will I do for your purposes?"

Wayne so much wished for an attorney. He had a strong sense that he and Jedediah would not speak the same language, that there were sure to be complications beyond those normally expected when an adversary was not a lawyer.

"Yes, I suppose so. You probably know why I am here." Jedediah nodded understandingly.

"I assume you are here to talk about Hell." Amused and gracious. "Shall we go up to my office?"

The "office" was a single room a bit larger than Wayne's two rooms combined. Two four paneled windows allowed a view of Eastern Avenue and the mirroring facades across the way. A beige carpet excessively worn. A solitary scuffed black leather executive desk chair out of place at one end of the room, the only other item a green steal two drawer filing cabinet behind the chair.

"I hope you don't mind if I take my chair. It is what I am accustomed to. My flock uses the floor, but you are invited to sit on the cabinet there. I can swivel the chair to face you." Jedediah's tenor voice resonated softly in the empty room. His placid expression seemed genuine, but the pose he assumed after "taking" his chair suggested an austerity that was somewhat contrived. Wayne was very anxious, doubtful that the interview would be productive.

"You and your followers are causing serious harm to my client." Jedediah appeared to show sincere concern.

"I am not pleased to hear that," he said. "We do not wish to cause harm. Quite the contrary. We wish to promote joy."

"Whatever your intention may be, you are preventing my client from opening his business. You do not have the right to do that." Jedediah trying to envelope Wayne with benevolent indulgence.

"Yes, your client wishes to open the gates of hell. I believe that we do have the right to prevent that, to protect the innocent from descending into the lair of the devil. You speak of harm, Mr. Wayne. What of the harm to be suffered by those children of God who are lured into this place of evil? Do you think we can stand idly by while the demon destroys the souls of good people?"

"But it's just pretend. Just a club. Just entertainment. Not going to harm anyone."

"I wish it were as you expect it to be. You seem to be a fine man, Mr. Wayne. A righteous man. But is it not possible that you are looking at this 'club', as you call it, with the eyes of its advocate?   Perhaps your subjective perception betrays your objective knowledge."

Wayne beginning to sense the seeds of exasperation. "It does not matter how I perceive it. My client has the right to do it regardless of what I think of it. Or what you think of it. And you and your followers are breaking the law by obstructing his activities."

"What law do you refer to? Certainly not the criminal law. We are demonstrating most peacefully. Several police officers have come by. Some even have chatted with us. No warnings. No orders to disperse. No arrests."

"No, but if necessary, I will file a petition asking the court for an injunction by which the court will order you and your followers to stay away from my client's business. If you disobey the order, I will get another order for you to be charged with civil contempt and possibly arrested. That is why I am here – to avoid that. Like you, I prefer to work things out peacefully."

Jedediah stared into Wayne's eyes for a long moment, his expression unchanged, as if he were looking for something inside Wayne's mind. Then he closed his eyes and chuckled. "You realize, don't you Mr. Wayne, that you literally are the attorney from hell?" Letting the rib sink in. "That's quite a reputation to have. Sure you want to go there?"

No, Wayne most definitely did not want to go there. This case was flashing warnings as bright as a high intensity strobe light. His inclination to abandon it was very powerful and he had to use all his force of will just to complete the interview.

"So there's no chance of resolving this? Can you perhaps find another way to protest?" Jedediah smiled and shook his head.

"I don't believe what we are doing is protesting, as that word is used traditionally. We are guardians. Perhaps protectors is a better term. We are shields, human shields, standing in the way of people who might otherwise succumb to the devil's invitation, his temptation. We cannot just write a letter to the editor or to our local congressman. Only our presence, and through us the presence of God, will achieve the objective."

"Ok, if that's the way it has to be .." Wayne sighed and stood up to leave. One last thought: "What if my client changes the name of the place?"

"He won't."

"How do you know? How can you possibly know that?"

"Trust me, Mr. Wayne. I know him." Jedediah's certainty, reflected in his supremely confident fixated eyes, disturbed Wayne and rolled a shudder down his spine. Now he was desperate to get out.

"Ok. But just hypothetically, so I can try."

"Maybe. But he will more likely abandon the project before choosing a new name. But maybe." Forgetting to shake Jedediah's hand, he hurried towards the door at the far end of the room, jumped down the stairs, and burst out into the happy sunlight.

Driving back to the office he listened to a radio report about the stunning revelation that the new President, Adrianna

Hernandez, had issued a statement confirming the truth of a reporter's claim that she was born outside the United States. Apparently, her mother had not been well enough to travel to Tucson, where her husband was waiting, before she went into labor. Hernandez thus was born in Cananea, Mexico and brought to Arizona when she was three-days old.

The statement further declared that Hernandez had known nothing of these facts until her parents finally disclosed them to her after the story broke. The President concluded by saying that she and her advisers would be assessing the ramifications of these facts and the native born citizen clause in Article II of the Constitution before announcing any decisions concerning her response.

4

The blizzard of news and opinion about the President's predicament intensified overnight. Calls for her to resign immediately came shrill and supercilious from many quarters. She is not eligible. In fact, her presidential status is null and void. Simple as that.

But some counseled a more deliberate process. Let the President state her intentions. Then take action if necessary. What action? many asked. What happens if she will not resign? The Constitution itself offers no procedure to enforce its presidential eligibility provisions. What power can order a remedy?

Shutting this chaos out of his mind, Wayne sat at his desk preparing to draft papers in support of an injunction against the New Life Congregation of Awakening. The court must protect the gates of Hell, he imagined as the opening line. Enjoin the righteous from interfering with the right of the wicked to enter and the privilege of the Devil to torment them.

But Mr. Wayne, what is Hell all about? How can we protect it if we don't know what it is? No one knows what Hell is all about, your honor. No one who has been there has ever come back. How do you know that, Mr. Wayne? Is it not possible that someone has been there, come back, and not talked about it? What do you expect: Hi. Just got back from Hell. Fine place. Fragrant rose gardens. Gently flowing streams. Tastiest abalone I ever had.

Kat interrupted his daydreaming with the mail. All junk – except for one piece that Wayne was now puzzling over. It was a strange item that appeared to be sheets of rough yellow paper folded and bound with a red wax seal. Wayne remembered seeing similarly sealed papers many years before in a postal history exhibit. Above the seal was an illegible scrawl that Wayne guessed to be the sender's address. On the other side appeared Wayne's name and address in the same handwriting but legible enough to make out.

"Have you heard about all the demonstrations? Spontaneous crowds. Most of the major cities. Huge numbers in some cases. Don't know if there is anything in Baltimore, but I would sure be there if I could. Maybe in DC." Noting that Wayne was preoccupied with a letter, she sighed and left the room.

Wayne wondered if the letter might be trouble, a sense that bothered him frequently lately, probably because of the turn his practice was taking. But if trouble was looking for him it would find him one way or another. Besides the modern world offered many more lethal methods to inflict harm than could possibly result from a package put together as a replica of 18th century correspondence. He broke the seal, releasing two pieces of musty paper. On one side of the top paper was this letter hand-written, the addressee's name written by a hand different from the rest:

Dear Mr. Wayne

I hope this finds you in good health and spirits.

I write on a matter of grave importance to the United States. This is a country that I was instrumental in founding and, even though my efforts have been forgotten and my achievement disregarded, I remain very proud of my contribution and I wish whole-heartedly for the continued success and prosperity of this great nation.

Consequently, I am deeply troubled by recent events. For so many years I have held my tongue while those who rule the country have treated the Constitution of the United States as if its words had been chiseled in stone by God, not to be tampered with except by the unwieldy and archaic process God himself also decreed by permanent inscription. But I can no longer contain my dismay.

Those of us who gathered in Philadelphia in the summer of 1787 never intended or imagined that the document we crafted would be unalterable or the final word unto eternity. We did it in three months for God's sake! While some may have envisioned a more lasting product, I, for one, was motivated by a spirit of pragmatism, rooted in the simple need to get something set up so that the nation could rest on a firm foundation while it commenced life. I, and I am certain my colleagues, assumed that future generations would revise our work as the country and its society evolved and that the constitution we wrote would be succeeded by one or more new constitutions in future years.

A salient example of the absurd reverence in which the literal wording of the constitution is held concerns the clause prohibiting any but a natural born citizen to be eligible to serve as president. This clause was quite unremarkable at the time. None of us paid any attention to its effect. Mr. Washington asked that it be included and so it was. There was no debate and no discussion. We did not dwell on it because it seemed obvious that the clause would survive only as long as its usefulness. There was little doubt among us that the nation and the world might develop such that modifying or eliminating the clause, or simply ignoring it, would become wise. That this day has come is too evident for dispute.

There are many other provisions in the constitution as I – we -- wrote it that now are anachronistic at best or even stupid. The process for electing a president, for example. The People can vote for one person to be their president, but the electoral college process gives someone else the job. This was my idea. It was the closest to a true expression of the People's will that I could convince my aristocratic colleagues to accept. But it has long since become merely a nefarious device for thwarting the People's will. And once this president is inaugurated the People are stuck with him for four long years no matter what he does or does not do.

Something must be done. You are the man to do it.

Yours very sincerely,

James Wilson

The name immediately linked Wayne's mind to Patrick Marius. But other than that he had no clue as to what the letter meant or what its purpose could be. Someone wrote a letter and purported the author to be a man dead for more than two centuries. And sent it to Frank Wayne. Why? Was it Marius, the only person he had ever heard mention the name James Wilson? If so, what was the point? What was he supposed to do with it?

Throw it in the trash; that's what. The letter indeed would be trouble, if he let it. Better to dispose of it immediately and treat the episode like it never happened. He had work to do.

Still he knew he could not just ignore it. The letter would distract him even more from the waste basket. He should at least see if the author can be identified. He called Kat back into his office.

"We need to find out who sent me this weird letter. It may be the work of a professor I had in law school. Crazy ass dude. Obsessed with James Wilson."

"Who is James Wilson?"

"Depends on who you ask, I guess. Marius thought he was the guy who actually wrote the constitution and never got credit for it."

"You mean he's dead?"

"Couple of hundred years dead. Wilson I mean. Don't know about Marius. Last thing I heard he was arrested in Philadelphia. Threatened some clerk with a pencil."

"So what do ya think is up with this letter? And why you?"

"No friggin' idea. We need to figure out where he is and what he's doing. See if I can contact him. Work on it please. Patrick Marius. Lived in Towson. Taught at Baltimore Law School and some other places. Arrested in Philly about seven years ago. Shouldn't be too hard to track him down. To get some good leads anyway. Maybe start with the Pennsylvania arrest records."

Scanning around his office after Kat left Wayne grew anxious, a slight chill in his feet, his laptop humming like distant bees touching off annoying tingling through his back. The scene was as it had been for years: Boxes stacked like sediment marking the time that had passed, the oldest gently crushed at the bottom where they had sat since the Bannion auto fraud matter concluded twelve years ago.

First and last auto fraud. Client brought in some kind of auction report that noted frame damage to the BMW 320i she bought used from a Finksburg dealer. No one told me about it, she said. No frame damage, dealer told Wayne. No frame damage, dealer told the court. No real frame damage, auction company told the court. Just holes drilled to install a trailer hitch.

The 1935 wall photograph of the Baltimore County Courthouse in Towson framed in glass, now greasy and cracked after 15 years hanging in the same spot.

Piled against the metal green surplus lateral file cabinet were three retired Dell tabletop computers that had been waiting more than five years to be recycled, subject to Wayne's senseless fear that someday he might need something that was stored on their hard drives. Like maybe photos of his client's surgery scars and the abdominal binder he was forced to wear after a surgeon at Mercy Medical had lacerated his spleen trying to drain a pleural effusion.

You never know, Wayne's lizard brain whispered whenever he noticed the computers. Why don't you just transfer the files to your laptop? Kat asked him periodically. Yeah, that's what I should do, he responded each time. Then, contemplating that he would have to hook the units to monitors, find a keyboard, connect to a power source, find a floppy disk, figure out what he wanted to transfer … it never happened.

For the Historical Society fracas the authorities let Marius off with a misdemeanor assault charge and time served.

Kat also was able to find a blurb posted on a website called falsefounders.com. The site contained several one paragraph summaries, cryptically written with haphazard grammar and random punctuation, of various conspiracy theories concerning the American founders.

For example, it turns out that the "real George Washington

was killed off = when at the Battle of the Monongahela //the man which later becomes *Father of his Country+ imposter born to Wales >> Reginald Blumberry that served in " 44th Regiment of Foot // General Braddock]]: instant transplant... colonies @@@Washington's wig, clothing, identity."

And "James Madison = woman had accident >> penis chopped to jealous of other men married lesbian for sex in ass from slave brothers and Charles Pinckney."

And "Alexander Hamilton real name Joseph Bit]] opium dealer to Martha and Abigail A. the prostitute doing tricks as John does the country // stole gold from Morris that shipped to Jamaica offered to Burr for silence re homosexual."

And "James Wilson = THE Committee of Detail // hand writing constitution ... saving pompous no good committee asses Saturday with convention expecting draft Monday >> hounded dead by debt while slave masters be honored founders."

"How do you know this is Marius?" Wayne asked Kat. "I mean it's his bit all right."

"Click the little flag at the end." Wayne did and a tiny pop-up window displayed the words "Contributor: Patrick Marius, American Heretic."

"Let's search this moniker." He googled "Patrick Marius" and "American Heretic". Three items came up. The first one linked to a short news item on a local news blog from Monmouth County, New Jersey:

"An adjunct instructor of history at Brookdale Community College yesterday was escorted off the campus by college police after he allegedly disrupted another teacher's class with shouting and threatening hand gestures. The instructor, identified as Patrick Marius, had been hired only a week before as a temporary fill-in for a history professor who went on leave for treatment of stomach cancer.

"The incident occurred during a class on United States

history to 1800. According to reports from students, the teacher had been in the middle of her lecture when Marius burst in and started shouting at her from the back of the class. The only words they could recall were 'That's a lie and you know it' and something about 'a filthy slave trader'. The students said he did not advance any further, but pointed at the teacher and, according to one student, gestured as if pulling a trigger.

"Marius apparently then abruptly stopped speaking and stood silently looking around the classroom like he had not realized until that point where he was. As the police rushed in and grabbed him he began to cry and mutter 'I'm sorry' several times before he was dragged away. In a statement issued later the campus police reported that Marius identified himself only as "the American Heretic".

"Oh my god," Kat said reading over Wayne's shoulder. "This guy's a freak."

"Maybe."

"Maybe?" Getting excited. "Maybe? He needs to be put away somewhere."

"Not for us to judge." But Wayne was not as calm as he wanted Kat to think. A tiny tumor of fear had begun to pulse in his gut. Not that he feared Marius exactly. He was still pretty sure that the American Heretic would not hurt anyone, physically at least. However his intuition about future events was enflamed. He sensed that somehow Marius was going to affect his career, or even his life, in some profound way.

Reluctantly, he clicked on the next google result. This one linked to an announcement posted on a site maintained by a group called "American Association for Constitutional Revision": "The Wilmington, Delaware chapter of the AACR is pleased to announce that Patrick Marius, aka the American Heretic, will speak on Sunday, November 12, at 5 p.m., at the home of the chapter's president, located at 1415 North Union Street, in

Wilmington. Marius, who is known to AACR members for his controversial views on the genesis of the American government, will speak on "'The Shame of American Historians: Their Cowardly Treatment of James Wilson'".

Wayne could not find anything indicating the year of the event and there appeared to be no post-talk report, so he asked Kat to get in touch with the AACR to obtain more information.

While she did that he clicked on the final of the three items. He came to a page from the site of a radio station broadcasting out of Harrisonburg, Virginia. On it was a transcript of the conversation "between early morning host Candace Dunston and an agitated caller who labeled himself the American Heretic."

"Good morning. You are on with Candace. What is your name please?"

"I am the American Heretic."

"Interesting. Is that some sort of stage name?"

"That is who I am."

"Ok. Take it easy. Now are you sure you're not an American heretic. Surely you're not the only one."

"Apparently I am."

"Why do you call yourself the American Heretic?"

"Because I know and denounce the fraudulent history accepted by scholars as the truth. I know who the so-called founders really were. I denounce them as false and as despicable slave masters, who chiseled racism into the cornerstone where it still--"

"Whoa. I gotta stop ya there AH. That's some pretty nasty stuff. Is that what you called to say?"

"I am trying to find anyone who will listen. I thought you might. Let me ask you a question. Who was the father of the constitution?"

"That's an easy one. If I didn't know that more than one of my college profs would let me hear about it. You are talking about Madison. James Madison."

"James Madison was nothing but a god damn slave master! Owned more than 100. Never freed them. A devil who conjured up the evil three-fifths compromise, then stole credit for the constitution from the real author."

"Who was?"

"James Wilson"

"Who?"

"You are just as ignorant as all the rest. Jesus Christ! I should go down there and teach you and all your dumb ass colleagues something even if I have to pound your heads into the wall!"

"Don't like your language or your threats. Cutting you off." An asterisk directed the reader to a footnote advising that the real name of the caller was Patrick Marius.

Kat reported that the AACR event had occurred the previous year, that only two people attended, that Marius showed up but refused to speak to just two people, and that there were no plans to reschedule the event. The person she spoke to had no idea where he was now. The only address Brookdale College had for Marius was a post office box in Red Bank, New Jersey.

So Wayne did something that was decidedly out of character for him: He put out a message on a social media site maintained by the Baltimore Law School for its alumni asking if anyone knew what had become of Patrick Marius. About five hours later he received the answer.

5

The Pennsylvania State Hospital for the Insane opened in Norristown, 21 miles north of Philadelphia, in 1880. A two-hour drive from Baltimore on I-95 and I-476. Now called the

Norristown State Hospital, it consists of "232 well-tended acres, flush with an assortment of mature hardwoods and pines that sway above winding pathways, office space with parking, a bustling greenhouse, a couple of ball fields, a trout stream ..."

Wayne passed through all the pastoral serenity without noticing a bit of it. As directed, he headed towards Building 51, the Male Disturbed Building, built in 1937 to house the criminally insane, now still housing the insane, but the "criminals" are held in that unit which the modern mental health profession calls the "Forensic Center."

Not surprisingly, 51 is a locked facility, surrounded by a 14-foot razor-wire fence. Reinforced windows with metal grates. Red brick and cinder block. For visitors, special metal doors, guards, and metal detectors.

Once inside Wayne's first impression was the smell: A noxious mixture of urine accumulated and fermented for decades, musty ammonia and Lysol, some kind of super-powerful bleaching agent, and a nauseatingly sweet air freshener. Similar to the smell of the mortuary after three of Wayne's cousins threw up during the viewing for his grandfather. His first breath of it was almost painful.

Then there was the sound: A continuous hum of voices echoing from the depths. Sorrowful moaning, monotonous chattering, one shouting something about "the japs", another singing a looping medley of television show theme songs – "come an listen to my story 'bout a man named Jed .. Monday Tuesday happy days ... keep them doggies rollin' ... who I am is who I want to be ..."

The staff watched amused as Wayne absorbed the scene. "Who you looking for?" one asked him. "Patrick Marius" he replied, trying to take short breaths.

Someone said "Is the Heretic still in 412?" Apparently receiving an affirmative, a burly fellow in white pants and a loose green shirt motioned for Wayne to follow him. They walked slowly along a narrow bright white corridor and through metal doors opened remotely by a scowling nurse sitting to the side at a raised desk before a window opened to the other side. Once inside, another scowling nurse asked Wayne what he had brought with him. Besides his wallet, keys, and cell phone, just a small pad of paper and a pen.

"No cell phone," she declared and held her hand out for it. "And no pen."

"I need the pen. To write notes. I am here to get information." She shook her head and intensified the scowl. Then said to Wayne's escort: "Who's he going to see?"

"The Heretic." With no indication that she was making an exception, she nodded for them to proceed. More metal doors opened remotely and they were in some kind of ward where maybe twenty patients and a few hospital workers sat in groups, some playing card games, others drawing, while three gaunt and frightened gentlemen paced from one end of the ward to the other and back again to start over. When they saw Wayne they each gasped in fear and retreated in panic to the end they had just started from, crouching there and staring at him.

One of the card players jumped up and approached Wayne. A tall, glass-eyed man of about 50, with very thin silver hair. "How do you do, partner?" he said with an exaggerated Texas drawl.

"Just passing through," Wayne's escort told him, gently blocking his progress with a beefy left arm.

"Just tryin' to make the feller's acquaintance. Looks like a right fine friend. Maybe you can help me steer these here no gooders. Ain't had no hands round here lately. Boys getting' outta control." He followed and kept jabbering as the three of them crossed the ward. "Who ya here to see anyway?"

"Don't worry about that," the escort told him as they came

up to another set of metal doors.

"We got all kinds in here, you know. Killers, men of the cloth, generals, even a Heretic." Wayne glanced at him. "That's it, ain't it? Yer goin to see the Heretic. Well good luck. He don't like nobody. Cept one other feller. Some old dead guy name o' Wilson or something. Won't talk 'bout nothin' else."

The closing metal doors shut him off after Wayne passed through. On he and the guide went along another bright white corridor, past a series of steel doors with tiny windows, past muffled muttering and moaning and sometimes incoherent shouting.

They arrived at 412.

From inside came a sound that seemed like snoring in its rhythm and guttural source, but also speech of a sort, words, though not intelligible words. He looked in at the door his escort unlocked and held open for him. He could see nothing past a very bright light shining at him.

"Professor Marius?" he said tentatively. The only response was more of the same sound he heard in the all. "Professor Marius, do you remember me?" The sound continued, then stopped abruptly.

"Of course I remember you, you filthy scoundrel." Marius was trying to yell, but there was something sandy in his throat that muffled the voice. "How dare you appear before me unannounced. I won't have it!" Still unable to see the face, Wayne hovered nervously in the light.

"This is a new low, even for you. Confound it, why can't you leave me alone. I'll pay the god damn bill when I can. Maybe. You charge me 50 bucks for a kidney pie and expect me to run over with the money. It's not like that anymore Washburn. The stage coach is teetering on the cliff. The fullbacks have hit the line. All in the sewer. All in the sewer." With that the sand finally ground the voice quiet and Wayne stepped forward.

"Not who you think it is, I guess," he said, trying assurance. Now he saw the face. Or rather what there was of a face buried in beard and sheets and pillows. Shrunken gray eyes, frightened at first, then slowly focusing, concentrating, recognizing? He lifted his head slightly as if to begin the sitting up process, but nothing more came of it.

"I confess that you look familiar. You are one of the taxing authorities. No, Senator Craddick. That's it. Senator, how nice of you to come. Who's chairing the committee while you're out humoring the old lunatic?"

"No, not Senator Craddick professor. Frank Wayne. I was a student and then--"

"Wayne!" Marius stammered. "Frank Wayne. I'll be a son of a bitch." The eyes seemed to liquefy, and the head fell back.

"Good to see you sir."

"Oh my god. Is it? In this catastrophic condition? You are kind, but I don't believe a word of it. Still I welcome you to the mad house. You are a courageous one."

Wayne laughed and pulled a folding chair up to the bedside. "So you don't mind if I stay and chat with you a bit?"

"Chat all you want. But remember that every minute you're here you do so at your own risk. I cannot be responsible for your safety." Wayne glanced around the room. Except for a walker folded and parked in a corner, a couple of other health contraptions, a small dresser, a floor lamp, and the bed, the room was quite barren. The only window was shut and covered by a metal shield.

"Looks to me like the only potentially dangerous thing in here is you."

"How feeble the senses of man." He studied Wayne intently, trying so hard to find something through his eyes still squinting from the light. The escort remained waiting in the doorway. Marius eyed him suspiciously. "We can't talk with the authorities monitoring."

Wayne convinced the man to leave, but only after he had shown Wayne a button he could press if help was needed. Wayne closed the door behind him.

"The plow man is digging up the bottles. But the wine from the grapes of wrath must be bitter." Then, motioning for Wayne to bend close: "Turn off the damn tape recorder."

"No tape recorder," Wayne responded.

"You are a fucking liar! I won't have it." Every time Marius erupted in anger like this it seemed that he spent his last reservoir of energy for it. He again tried to raise himself but collapsed again into the pillows and sheets.

"I did not come here to record you." Marius tried to look skeptical, then seemed overwhelmed with sorrow. He sobbed very softly.

"Of course you didn't," he mumbled pitifully. "No one ever does. No one wants to hear from a ridiculous old lunatic." It was so pathetic that Wayne thought he too might start to sob. Better get to the point.

Pulling the letter from his pocket he carefully unfolded it and held it where Marius could see it if he chose to. He didn't. "What's that?" he cried, cringing away from the paper.

"It's a letter I received the other day. I suspect that it came from you. I'm here to find out."

Marius stared incredulously into Wayne's eyes for a brief moment, then burst out in wheezing, gasping laughter. "You suspect that it came from me, you say. That's hilarious." The activity took its toll. His wispy frame was seized again, and he lay his head back down to let the gagging run its course. Then he raised a finger and wagged it, whispering "Not from me, my friend. I write no letters."

After a few minutes Marius again motioned for Wayne to put his ear close. "Did you say you were a student in one of my classes?" This confirmed, Marius struggled to cup one hand by his lips and whispered "he's here ya know."

"Who's here?"

"Jesus Christ! You said you were in my class." Marius gasped with short angry breath. Wayne solved the mystery for himself.

"You don't mean James Wi--"

"Of course that's who I mean."

"Why do you think he's here?"

"I've seen him. I've talked to him."

Wayne tried again. "Professor, this letter purports to be from James Wilson himself. That's why I'm here. That's why I thought maybe you did it."

Marius' eyes seemed to widen and protrude at Wayne. "Maybe he did write it. How should I know? But I –" pointing to his chest – "I did not write any letters."

Now Wayne was growing frustrated and a little angry, searching for some way to get through the miasma to a region of the lunatic's brain that remembered. "Could you just read it? See if any of it is familiar to you?"

Marius suddenly bent forward and tried to grab Wayne's throat. "No! I will not read it!" he managed to shout, before falling back into his pillows. "You son-of-a-bitch come here," he wheezed, "and charge me with forging a document in his hand. Shame on you!"

Exasperated and ready to leave, Wayne folded the letter and put it back in his pocket. "I am sorry to have bothered you," he said quietly.

At which Marius began to cry. And he reached out to clasp Wayne's arm. "I'm sorry. I'm sorry. I'm sorry. It was only natural for you, getting a letter from Wilson, to think of me. I am so grateful that you remembered. The next time I see him I will ask if he wrote you a letter. I know that he is very disturbed about things that are happening with the government. Maybe that's what he wrote you about?"

Wayne nodded, so touched that he could not speak, wondering what it could be like in the mind of this horribly confused and demented man, suffering through violent bursts of anger quickly followed by a whimpering collapse so pathetically contrite.

"Before you go," Marius whimpered. "I cannot read – my eyes are not so good – but tell me, in the letter, did Wilson ask you for something?"

"Only to fix everything."

"He is very upset. Won't talk about anything besides the government. Wishes he never had anything to do with it." And, after a deep pause: "What are you going to do?"

Finally understanding the futility of his mission, and fighting a nauseating depression of helplessness, Wayne briefly considered but dismissed any further resort to reason. There was no artery to rationality here. If some isolated, remote section of Marius' mind still recognized reality Wayne was not going to reach it. He was confident now that Marius was responsible for the letter, but had no way to know from how far back in the progress of mental deterioration it had come. At that moment, with Wayne standing beside the bed and Marius waiting for the answer, his eyes pleading for help, there seemed no point in contesting the illusion.

"I don't know," he finally said. "I will need to think about it. I don't know if there is anything I can do."

"False!" Marius shouted with all the charge he had left. "You can do it! You are a great man! This country is depending on you! You must do it!" And with that Marius collapsed into unconsciousness.

6

Of course there was nothing Wayne could do. He might just as well try out for the Baltimore Ravens as waste his time in any activity related to politics. For one thing, politics is an inherently social behavior; he was not of that species. He could be friendly, even engaging, when it was necessary or useful. But he considered that part his dark side, never likely to fire any enthusiasm or joy.

There also was the sour futility he saw as an inevitable byproduct. No one ever really accomplished anything in politics; the best result usually was just sand moved from one fill to another or poured into bags so as to become a form people believed would protect them from a flood. Wayne thought of politics as a mere pastime, something to disguise the passage of time, like watching baseball.

Certainly there was little chance of making any money at it. Maybe if one had the skill and nerve for corruption. But although he considered himself intelligent enough, Wayne definitely lacked the nerve for the kind of risks that might bring some return. He was a decidedly under the radar kind of guy.

So he was not about to embark on some Don Quixote style crusade to change the American government. No, he had real work to do. He had to get the doors to Hell open. The unfolding drama in Washington he would watch, as he always had, from the bleachers, too far away for any of the protagonists to hear him even if he was carried away enough to call someone a "bum".

He filed the "James Wilson" letter at the back of a drawer containing old continuing legal education materials.

Next he began an email to Kemal. Drafting the papers, he explained. Need some information. First, however, he conveyed what he thought was precious advice: Change the name. Simplest course of action. Pick one of the many other words that signify the same place   Tartarus, for example. The Greek equivalent – "a deep, gloomy place, a pit or abyss used as a dungeon of torment and suffering."   Or the Jewish Gehinnom.   Or Jahannam, the Islamic version.   To be clear, Wayne was not insisting on a new name; he would proceed with the lawsuit even if its object was to protect Hell. It was just that a new name would be considerably more expedient.

To that end he needed proof that the demonstrators were causing harm to Kemal, so Wayne asked for some statements about specifically what bad things had happened so far and what was certain to happen if he tried to open the establishment with the demonstrators still there.

He also needed some evidence to show that Kemal's model of Hell was a component of his and his associates' genuinely held religious beliefs. What religion? How did they practice?   How did their Hell relate to it?   Who would be participating, i.e., entering Hell? In sum, Wayne said he needed every bit of information Kemal could provide without describing what actually would transpire within.

Kemal answered the first issue within 30 minutes: No way! Absolutely no change to the name! And he was not willing to discuss it further. If Wayne had a problem with it Kemal would excuse him from the contract and look for a new lawyer. He promised to respond later regarding the information Wayne requested.

So Wayne and Kat went for an early lunch. The Yak Shack. No real yak on the menu, just sandwiches with Himalayan related names. Kat ordered the Gangtok, Wayne the Rohtang, and they sat at one of the small tables too close to the television, which was blasting CNN at a volume pre-set for the much more crowded Noon hour.

As always, the news team was covering "breaking news". "Three or perhaps four squads of very high-profile legal minds are meeting as we speak in various locations around Washington, Virginia, and Maryland. They are devising strategy for bringing an outcome favorable to their clients from the morass into which the national government has sunk since the revelation about President Hernandez' place of birth."

"Breaking news?" Kat said, popping open a can of soda. "That's the same crap they've been saying for days – or is it weeks – I have lost track." Wayne smiled and gnawed his sandwich. "Hey, when they say 'high profile' they really mean incredibly expensive, don't they? Why can't you get in on some of that action? You're as good as most of those knuckleheads."

Through a mouthful of lamb, onions, and pine nuts Wayne tried to explain about Harvard and Yale and Princeton, about wealthy, prestigious law firms, about legal royalty who did work for the powerful, and about bottom-feeding law grunts like him who did not. He did work for clients like Hell.

"Yeah yeah yeah. I've heard all that from you so many times before. I don't think I ever knew someone who sold himself short like you." Wayne genuinely appreciated the buttering up. No one else did it anymore. Take a good word wherever you find it, even from an obviously biased employee.

The place was filling with bodies now. And loud chatter. So he did not hear it the first time. Only after the person shouted "hey Frank Wayne" again and came close enough did Wayne recognize Lamont Burke, a client he had helped a couple of times, the most recent probably two or three years ago.

Burke owned a small nightclub in the Inner Harbor area of Baltimore. His legal issues had not been much, an employment matter and a little trouble with the liquor control people. But he and Wayne had often fell into discussions, or sometimes even debates, about current events, most having nothing whatsoever to do with them. An opinionated extrovert, Burke rarely ran into Wayne without baiting him on some topic that was then the subject of controversy. There being only one such topic in the air as the two shook hands in The Yak Shack, it was hardly surprising that Burke broached the presidential dilemma.

"Now Frank, I know you got something to say about this crazy mess with the president."

"I don't know about that, Lamont. But I know *you* got something to say about it."

"Well yes and no. I mean I know what common sense tells me. But I just don't know enough about the meat of the matter. I guess it's a constitutional law thing and that's pretty much outta my range. But you probably got it all figured out."

Wayne was stunned by the discourse that then came out. Thoughts that apparently had been percolating in his semi-conscious mind without his acknowledgement suddenly assembled into coherence and burst forth. Was this him talking?

"Well the thing is Lamont, it's not really a constitutional law thing at all. Constitutional law concerns mostly construction of the words in the constitution and how they are to be applied to certain circumstances. As I see it, what is happening here is different. The words are not unclear. They are not ambiguous. President Hernandez was born in Mexico. Thus she is not a natural born citizen. Under the plain language of the constitution she is not eligible to be president."

"You know that's bullshit," Burke said, and Wayne realized that others were eavesdropping on the conversation and approving his reaction.

"It's not bullshit. That's what the law says. But that's why this is not a constitutional law question. The issue for me is whether we are going to get rid of a president solely because those words are written there. Are we going to allow a few words that a few men more than two hundred years ago whimsically inserted into the document without any consideration dictate what the people can do now with respect to their president?"

Now more and more patrons of The Yak Shack were listening to him. His pulse was pounding, adrenalin ripping his gut. The feeling of being out on a tree limb and needing to grab the fruit before he could turn back and climb down.

"I am certain that the real author of the constitution would be flabbergasted and disgusted if he knew this had even become an issue. I am certain he would declare that if the law of the constitution requires the president to resign because she was born in Mexico three days before she came to America then the constitution is wrong and must be changed or simply ignored!"

A few of the onlookers clapped as Wayne sat down. Burke folded his arms and looked at Wayne like he just hit a three-point shot to win the game. "Damn," he said. "Where did that come from?"

Wayne grimaced sheepishly and shook his head. "I don't know. I haven't really even been paying attention to the news." Some of the strangers joined in Burke's laughter.

"Well man, I wonder what you would say if you had been paying attention."

Kat was staring at Wayne trying to figure out whether he was the boss she came in with. Then as they walked back to the office, she repeated Burke's comment: "Where did that come from? Never heard anything like that from you."

Still wondering himself, Wayne shrugged and glanced around to see where the answer might be. "I guess it's on my mind more than I realized. It's because of Marius. And Wilson. I mean Marius."

Back to Hell. While waiting to hear back again from Kemal, he tried to begin writing a complaint. But he had to leave too many blanks for the information he did not have yet and soon gave up.

The phone. Kat: "There's a lady on the line who says she was just at the Yak place and heard you. Got the number from

Lamont Burke."

"Hello, this is Frank Wayne."

"Hi Mr. Wayne. My name is Kathy Black. I was just at The Yak Shack and overheard your wonderful speech. Have you got a couple of minutes?"

On the steering committee of a new group organizing for action on the presidential matter. Barely getting started. A few interested people met informally two nights ago to work on a game plan. Nothing concrete yet. Meeting again tonight. Would love to have him come if he has time.

Wayne tried to explain how the "speech", as she called it, was purely spontaneous, that he was not the civic rabble rouser type, just the opposite, that he did not feel capable of making much of a contribution, and, finally, that despite what he said at the Yak he did not believe there really was anything that could be done. Appreciate the invitation and sorry to be so negative.

Kathy Black assured him that he would not be making any commitment. It would help them tremendously just to hear what ideas he might have. They needed moral support from someone more knowledgeable than they are. One meeting, maybe half an hour or so, then no one would expect anything further. They would be using a conference room in a real estate brokerage about a mile from his office. Please think about it and come if you can.

Not about to waste his evening participating in an interminable debate about the wording of the group's mission statement, Wayne dismissed the idea and focused again on Hell. One meeting – right. He knew better how these things played out. Once he stuck his face inside the door he would be trapped for the duration. Groups like that, especially where there is a political objective, attached members like fly paper. And from the outset the hours of labor mushroom, consuming every minute he otherwise would devote to his chosen profession and cutting off the fees he desperately needed. He simply could not afford it. Let the wealthy lawyers work it out. After all, they probably are getting paid buckets of cash just to think about the problem, growing even fatter financially for doing what Kathy Black wanted him to do for nothing. Not even nothing. He surely would *lose* money. And for what? Exactly.

Now he became concerned about how long it was taking Kemal to get back to him. If the situation was truly that urgent why should it take more than an hour or so to put together the little bit of information Wayne requested. The longer the delay the less likely the court would be to consider the matter an emergency. You and your client waited this long to seek relief, Mr. Wayne, so doing a noticed motion on the regular calendar should not be a problem.

The phone.   Lindsay, whose case Judge Goliath had dismissed with a smile. Upset and frantic. "What the hell's going on?" she shrieked. "Why haven't I heard from you? Just that voice message from your bitch there saying the judge tossed the case. Why didn't you get more time? What am I supposed to do now?"

Wayne listened until the initial hysteria waned a bit. "Judge had had enough. You weren't there again. Nothing I could do."

"Don't give me that crap! I don't believe it. I told you what happened."

"Same thing that happened the first three times. Judge gave us four chances. Nothing I could do."

"Then maybe there's nothing I can do about your god damn bill! What the hell am I paying for? What am I supposed to do now?"

"I guess you can try to find another lawyer who might have better luck with the judge. There's nothing else I can do for you."

"Yeah, or find a lawyer to sue your ass for incompetence!"

Wayne wanted so much to hang up. But he managed to stay on the line until Lindsay did. Then he thought about the bottle of scotch waiting in one of his drawers. Did not succumb to the temptation. Just closed his eyes, took deep breaths, and let the tension settle. And imagine what other line of work he might take up, something where he could work eight hours until the whistle blew, then spend a blissful evening not thinking once about work. Something where he would not be responsible for other people's problems.

He called Kemal. "Mr. Wayne, I have to call you back." Loud voices in the background. A language he did not recognize. Apparently arguing. Wayne quickly reiterated the need for quick action and said he would be waiting.

The phone. Possible new client, Kat said. Beneficiary of a trust. Wanted to sue the trustees for mishandling it. They were using the money to pay medical bills for a young girl he was falsely accused of assaulting. They were conspiring with the girl's parents. Slam dunk case. Wayne would easily snag six figures in contingency fees. Cannot help you. Referral? Don't know anyone who did that kind of thing. Irate. What is it with you attorneys? If I had the fat wallet you would jump to help me. Whatever. Good bye.

Kat. Agitated. (Like everyone else today.) Have you heard? President Hernandez has scheduled an address to the nation for Thursday night, three days from now. They expect her to resign. We have to do something. You can do something. Your speech today. Do something with it.

"What can I do?" Wayne responded weakly, sensing some outrage but not enough.

Kat plopped into a chair and cried. "I don't know. I don't know. It's just so .. so .. messed up."

Women in tears was harder for Wayne than crazy old American heretics. Okay. Okay. He'll go to the meeting.

7

The room was packed. Wayne had to squeeze into a corner gap beside the end of a refreshment cabinet. Over the shoulders in front of him he could see eight people sitting in chairs around a table and maybe fifteen others standing behind them. More women than men, most still dressed for business, with a few young casuals, probably students. Every face was grave, some angry.

A sophisticated-looking woman occupying the head chair opposite to Wayne was just trying to quiet the hubbub. She seemed to measure her aggressiveness, clearly hoping to effect order out of what could have been a mob. But she did raise her voice slightly to be heard.

"We would like to get started ... if we can get everyone's attention." Once the last conversation died away: "Good evening and welcome to the second meeting of our as yet unnamed group. I am very happy to see many more new faces. My name is Kathy Black and I am the temporary chair, pending the adoption of a formal structure."

She glanced only at the sitting people as she spoke, obviously not accustomed to addressing more substantial audiences. "As you know I'm sure, our cause has reached a new urgency with the news this afternoon that President Hernandez will deliver a speech on Thursday, which many expect to announce her resignation. The goal of this group, and the others forming across the country, is to do whatever we can to prevent that from happening. That is our sole purpose. We are not here to discuss the issue or to provide information. It is too late for that. We are here for action. So if anyone here does not share this goal you will be wasting your time and ours by remaining."

A general murmur of affirmation followed, along with a few defections.

"Apparently the team of constitutional law experts the president's aides assembled has come up with exactly nothing to save her. As you know the Supreme Court will hold an extraordinary hearing on Friday to consider the lawsuits, but they may be moot by then. What I've heard is that it will not matter anyway since the president's lawyers have built up a huge bill but nothing else. So we need to decide what options for action remain. If we cannot come up with any then I guess we just go home and forget about it."

Three other seated persons, who seemed familiar to each other and Black, noted various instances of concerted action that had occurred in other large cities. The tone suggested that these demonstrations, letter writing campaigns, online petitions, etc. were decidedly ineffective, probably because they had no constitutional law authority supporting them.

Everyone who spoke exhibited a dampened and depressed spirit. Millions of people just like those assembled in that conference room vehemently believed that the discovery of the president's birthplace did not justify forcing her to resign, but, just like the constitutional law experts, there was no solid reason around which all these disparate groups could coalesce.

Wayne had plenty to say on the subject, but he knew if he opened his mouth he would become the center of the group's attention and he was not ready for that. He was there solely to see what the group was about. He did not intend to join it. However, his short stint as a spectator ended abruptly.

"Mr. Wayne!" Kathy Black exclaimed, finally noticing him hiding in the corner. "I am so glad you came." Twenty faces turned toward him. "Anyone who happened to be at The Yak Shack around noon today probably overheard Mr. Wayne's wonderful speech about all this. I was so taken I got his number and called him, urging him to come. I am so delighted that he did."

Wayne smiled and nodded but said nothing. Not a shy person normally, nevertheless he was very reticent about spouting his opinions, especially to strangers.

So Black persisted: "I don't think I could summarize your point very well, Mr. Wayne. Can you reiterate for us?"

His earlier performance had been purely spontaneous, a reaction to Lamont Burke's statement; it was not a well-considered expounding of anything. This open-ended invitation to speak was a different matter. Whatever he said now should be mentally organized and coherent.   Impossible in that circumstance.

"Well, as I explained on the phone," he mumbled, "I did not plan to say what I did. It just kind of came out. I haven't really analyzed the issue in any meaningful way. So I don't think—"

Kathy Black knew how to handle coy advocates. "Mr. Wayne, we need you to overcome your modesty. This is a crisis. If I recall correctly, you said something about it's not being a constitutional law problem. Am I right?"

"Yeah, I guess that's the gist of it." Speaking a bit more boldly. "Constitutional law is limited .. well, it's limited by the constitution. If the issue is what the constitution says and what its words mean and how they are to be applied to circumstances, then it's a constitutional law problem. In this case, for me, there is no such issue. The words are as clear as day. So is their meaning. They mean that president Hernandez is not eligible to be president."

The group grumbled and groaned. If it were not for Black, they might have shouted Wayne down. She waved them quiet and asked him to continue.

"So I guess my point is, to the extent I have one – again not a well thought out product – my feeling is that we should question why these words must control what we do just because the so-called founders inserted them in the document more than 200 years ago. Must we obey the words in the constitution even when they obviously are wrong and completely out of place today?"

A room of hushed and focused listeners, all attention intently directed at him. "I have reason to believe that the man who was the real father of the constitution, the man who actually wrote most of it, would consider what is happening a tragedy. He would say that the authority for the constitution itself is the people and if the people want Adrianna Hernandez to be their president, even though she was born in Mexico, that will of the people overrides those few words in the constitution."

Some were staring at him, struggling to believe that he really said what they just heard. One scholarly looking older man politely interrupted: "Who are you referring to when you say the real father of the constitution? Not James Madison?"

Channeling the American Heretic: "Not Madison. I'm talking about James Wilson."

Of course no one there knew who Wilson was. Wayne himself did not know much about him, so his explanations were not very satisfying. But, for the moment at least, this was not a big concern for anyone there. The question, raised by multiple persons almost at the same time, was what to do with the information Wayne had articulated. Wayne also was at a loss on this point.

Fortunately, Kathy Black was not. It turned out that her business was marketing, advertising, and publicity generally. "It is clear to me," she said, "that we must get attention, lots of it, and quickly. It may be impossible, but our only hope probably is to get noticed by Hernandez, or someone close to her. If only to be assured that she considers Mr. Wayne's notion before announcing her resignation."

Wayne stated the obvious: "But there is so little time."

"Mr. Wayne, you must not be a high-intensity user of social media."

With Black's leadership, the group coalesced into the Association for Saving the American President or ASAP. Notwithstanding his vehement protests, Wayne was proclaimed the president of ASAP. Black, who became the vice-president, assured him that he would be responsible only for composing or verbalizing the message, and would have nothing to do with organizing, outreaching, recruiting, generating publicity, or the like.

A sheet of paper was passed around for the new members of ASAP to provide contact information and to list any relevant skills or expertise. Some claimed expertise in web development, social media, and broadcast communications. Within an hour after the meeting began ASAP presented to the world an interactive website with optimal search access, multiple Facebook pages, Twitter, Instagram, and Reddit accounts, and many other electronic communication platforms.

Black instructed Wayne to compose an introductory message that he could announce in a video they would create that night for uploading to the website, the Facebook pages, and YouTube. Then they would email the video to every news and political information organization they could identify. She even had the nerve to tell Wayne he was looking tired and droopy and that he should go home, rest for 30 minutes, shave, take a shower, put on the nicest, cleanest suit he had, and come back to record the video. And was there any place he could get a haircut?

Once he had reset his jaw and sucked his dignity back up from the floor, he went off to obey her orders. There was a problem, however. He did not have a nice or a clean suit. Five years ago he had bought a wool-blend dark blue suit at Sears for $89.00. That was the newest and nicest in his closet. It was not clean. He could not remember when he last had it cleaned. But it would have to do.

A 30-minute nap, a shave, and a shower – no problem. Although he desperately preferred to stop at Ricky J's for a beer – or some scotch. Haircut? No way. His regular place had closed three hours ago, and he did not know of any other, much less one that would still be cutting. Besides he had been in for a trim not even a couple of months past. Couldn't be that bad.

Better consult with Kat. Mistake. She was so excited about his role in ASAP she invited herself to his place to help him. I know how to cut hair, she said. And how to make a suit look presentable.

Lying on his torn old couch he thought about the video message and did not sleep. Words and phrases flashed through his mind, images of Marius growing agitated in front of the class, writing the Wilson letter he didn't write, talking about his conversations with the ghost. Nothing would come together coherently.

This was not like drafting a legal brief. He had no template, no form to follow, no rules guiding and curbing his imagination. Just as well actually. If he was forced to wing it he would screw it up and be free. No longer a slave to the cause, he would be off the hook and able to get back to Hell.

In fact, why not just go over to Ricky J's, have a couple of scotch and sodas, maybe even three, so that he would be too drunk to make the video. He would call Kathy Black from there and confess. She would not be happy. But he would.

Just as he was locating his keys, however, someone knocked on his front door. Kat. Damn it! This was going to be difficult. And so it was. She promised him that if he did as he planned she would quit working for him. So much for getting drunk.

Kat trimmed his hair, brushed his suit, and hung it in the bathroom while he showered. When he drove back to ASAP he still had no idea what he was going to say, but he looked pretty good. Which Kathy Black and the other members still there confirmed.

Naturally, looking good made him feel better, more confident, ready to orate, even if a bunch of nonsense. Might need to record this a few times, he said. As many as you want.

They put him in a chair at the head of the conference table and set up the video recording device someone had obtained at the other end. Any time you're ready, Mr. Wayne, the nerd operating the thing said. Please call me Frank.

Take one. "Hello, my name is Frank Wayne. I am a lawyer practicing in Baltimore, Maryland. Through my work I have come to have knowledge about the United States Constitution, and I want to share it with you. This is garbage. Cut the recording please and I will try again."

Kathy Black: "You will want to grab people's attention right at the outset. Try getting straight to the point."

Take two. "Hello, my name is Frank Wayne. I am here to tell President Hernandez not to resign. It would not be – Crap. Not getting it. Must try again." Droplets of sweat formed behind Wayne's ears. It was past 11:00 p.m. There were maybe seven or eight people still there, either to encourage him or to see if he could really get it done.

Take three. "This is a time of crisis for the country. The future hinges on what happens this week. If the Daytona 500 goes off like last year we're screwed." No one laughed. A couple of indulgent smiles. Wayne thinking 'see I told you all. You need someone else to do this.'

Kathy Black: "I don't know about the rest of these folks, but I will stay here all night until you do something I know you are capable of." Oh my God. All night? Wayne had a day job to worry about. He probably would have to spend the morning arguing with Rafik Kemal about Hell. Maybe Jedediah as well.

Take four. "Madame President, please do not resign. The constitution cannot compel it. I have evidence that the dude who wrote it – shit, guess I can't say dude."

Now only four people: Wayne, Black, the video operator, and one of the web wizards waiting for the product. Black: "Shall we order some pizza? And coffee?" NO! Wayne did not sign on for an all-nighter. If agitation equaled motivation he was almost there. Almost in a zone.

Take five. "President Hernandez, you must not resign. For the sake of the United States, you must not resign. Regardless of the words inserted in the constitution more than two centuries ago, you must not resign. Because the People, who ordained and established that constitution, here and now ordain and establish that you are our rightful president and must not resign."

Feeling it. Strangely passionate.

"It does not matter whether the constitution deems you ineligible to be president because you were born in Mexico. The constitution was a rush job, a rough draft, hastily drafted by men who never intended it to be the final word. I have evidence of this in the hand of the man who was the principle author.

Possessed by the Heretic. Black and the others nodding and giving him thumbs up.

"Not James Madison. The American people should not forget that Madison, and many of his fellow so-called founders, owned hundreds of slaves. He bought and sold human beings. In addition to the natural born citizen clause that would bind the free people down the ages, Madison and his slave master colleagues also wrote into the constitution protections for their sordid human trafficking industry. And, despite enactments since, these provisions are still there, still a part of the constitution, and rendered ineffective only by amendments."

Unstoppable.

"The real author of the constitution was James Wilson. But

since he died alone and on the run from debt collectors, Wilson has been utterly blotted out of memory by historians, scholars, and politicians. I have evidence that Wilson would be shocked, disgusted, and depressed to learn that a person chosen by the People to be their president will be forced to resign solely because of a clause casually and hastily inserted in the constitution.

"My name is Frank Wayne. I am honored and proud to be the president of a brand new organization called the Association for Saving the American President or, as its acronym appropriately reads, ASAP. We believe that because of the present emergency it is finally time to recognize that many parts of the constitution, most immediately the natural born citizen clause, are ancient relics from a profoundly more primitive era of this nation, archaic vestiges of a nascent government struggling to take its first steps and stay on its feet long enough to become the great country that is today.

"We believe the People should use this crisis as a catalyst to finally call a new constitutional convention. This is a moment loaded with extraordinary possibility. We must not let it pass. Madame President, the first step is up to you."

Kathy Black on her feet, lunging over to hug him. "Fantastic," she said, her eyes wet. "Just wonderful."

PART V

President Adrianna Hernandez has stifled her ambivalence. She feels a sad sort of relief as she sits down for breakfast, still living alone in the White House, with only her sister Jennifer joining her for the morning meal that used to be such a special gathering of the family. The presidency is overwhelming. No one who has not had the job can possibly know what a monster it is. Already she can feel the skin along the side of her head starting to crack into lines and there are puffy patches under her eyes every morning. Nothing that a little make-up won't disguise, but still an unmistakable sign of the strain.

Yet now there is only relief. She slept better last night than she has for weeks. It is Tuesday morning. By Friday at Noon it will all be over. Thursday night she will speak to the nation and announce that because she is not a natural born citizen her lawyers have concluded that under the constitution she is not eligible to be president and so must resign the office, effective the following day at Noon eastern time.

It has taken many days of agonizing soul-searching and debate with advisers, family, friends, former presidents, and now even wealthier lawyers to reach this decision. She could have refused to resign, as many have urged. However, without some legitimate basis for doing so she feels that would be tantamount to an illegal seizure of power, the act of a despot and the ultimate betrayal of the People's trust.

The teams of legal experts employed on her behalf have come up with no genuine grounds for contending that the words of the constitution do not mean exactly what they quite unambiguously say. Consequently, with nothing to justify hanging on, and with plenty of personal motivation to let go, she finally told her staff yesterday to schedule the speech.

As she eats the bowl of oatmeal with new gusto Jennifer pokes at her food but does not eat it. Obviously depressed and not even trying to hide the signs of powerful emotion, Jennifer continues to cry as she has for most of the night. Hernandez feels enormous sympathy for her sister, but knows there is nothing more to say.

"You will arrange for the packing and all that?" Hernandez says quietly.

Jennifer just nods. "It's so unfair!" she says, sobbing. "I just can't believe it is happening."

Hernandez reaches over to grasp her sister's hand. "I am content. You will be too very soon."

Jennifer's cell phone vibrates, and she pulls it from her pocket to see who is calling, apparently hoping she need not answer. "Yes," she says, then listens. "A little late for that kind of thing." Rolls her eyes while holding the phone away from her ear. "How viral? … Wow … Ok, I'll take a look … Just to pad the misery."

Then to Hernandez as she hoists her laptop onto the table: "Seems there's something new. A new group and a video. Uploaded overnight and already viewed a gazillion times. Even a couple of the morning shows are talking about it."

Hernandez is not interested. She stands up to leave. "Great. No time for that crap now. You can let me know if it's anything."

Her schedule open until 9:30, Hernandez returns to her bedroom and lays in bed for half an hour reading newspapers and some memoranda she asked for a couple of weeks ago. The task she faces now is to determine what she can do in the next three days and what she must leave for Mike Jordan as her successor.

She has not communicated with him since their only meeting four days after the story of her birth in Mexico broke.

That meeting was not pleasant for either. While still deferential and respectful, Jordan displayed little tact and made it abundantly clear that he expected Hernandez to resign without delay. He even assured her that she would have whatever time she needs to move out of the White House. Warm and genial at the start, Hernandez quickly became icy and taciturn, telling Jordan only that neither of them should make hasty assumptions.

There would be further meetings. No way to avoid it. The smooth transfer of power requires their cooperation. At least there is some comfort in knowing that the reins of government will fall into the hands of someone who wants them.

The intercom device beside the bed buzzes. Jennifer. Hernandez probably should see the video if only in case she is asked about it. A direct appeal to her. Pretty compelling. And taking over the internet. Who did it? Guy named Frank Wayne. He's a lawyer in Baltimore. Figures. Yet another attorney. It's only three minutes.

Hernandez has a laptop beside the bed. She opens it and finds the video.

Not impressed. Not the first time anyway. Heard it all before. Guy wants her to launch another revolution. Even if there was the slightest wisdom in it, she does not have heart for the turmoil. She just wants to go home and hug her family, help her kids with their science fair projects, wash her husband's clothes, cook some empanadas.

However, as the minutes pass she realizes that ignoring this new appeal will not be so easy. The video is the phenomenon of the day. Everywhere she typically goes online – CNN, Politico, Washington Post, New York Times, CBS, Fox – there are links to it and stories about it "going viral" in amazingly short order and about a new organization with a name that is personally gratifying to her. Any moment now her communications director, press secretary, and who knows what other staff people, will insist on speaking with her about a response.

Response? Supposing she chooses to respond, what will she say? What is her "response"? Shrugging off a brief bout of anxious uncertainty, she watches the video again. This time she does not react so harshly. This Wayne fellow seems sincere at least. And she does not disagree with his view of the constitution or with his castigation of Madison as a hypocritical slave holder.

But he takes his complaints too far. The constitution is the foundation and frame for the government. Modifying any part of it always has required epochal effort. Furthermore, she swore to defend it, not revise it. And what would it mean for a president to insist on changing the constitution just so she can continue to be president.

She summons Jennifer. Who reports on multiple staff requests to confer with the president and a clamor for comment from outside the White House. "Did you see it?" she says.

"Yes," Hernandez responds in a tone of regret. "That's why I want to talk with you. I suppose we have to say something?"

"Well, I don't know that you have to say something formally. But at some point soon you will need to re-affirm your decision, to let it be known that the announcement on Thursday will proceed as planned … assuming that it will."

"That is my intention. Someone uploads a video that lots of people like. How can that affect what the president of the United States decides to do?" Jennifer looks quizzically at her sister, seeing some symptom of doubt in Hernandez' floating eyes.

"Yes, I supposed that's right," Jennifer said.

"Come on," Hernandez shoots back, irritated. "Don't just give me the 'yes I suppose you're right' treatment. I've got 50 people working here who can do that. Tell me what you think, damn it."

"You know what I think. We've been over it so many times."

"I mean this new thing. What do you make of it? Why should I give a damn about it?" Jennifer thinks her sister strangely impatient, considering her claim to having resolved the whole matter.

"Well, personally, I like their approach. I like it a lot. I agree with their premise. If the constitution requires that you resign because of where you were born, then the constitution is wrong. You should not resign; the constitution should be changed. But it's the popular reaction, not mine, that should get your attention."

"You mean we now live in a world where some nobody can affect the country's policies simply by making and uploading a video?"

"Consider the unique circumstances. When has there ever been a more momentous turning point?"

"Maybe that's my problem," Hernandez says tensely. "If I resign there will be no 'turning point' as you call it. The presidency will continue as it has all this time – subject to the constitution. If I don't resign that will be a turning point and who knows whether for good or evil. The burden is too much!"

Hernandez covers her face with her hands and chokes down the urge to cry. Both are silent for several minutes.

"I'm sorry," Hernandez finally whispers. "Just when I think I am past all this ... Do you think there is any point to conferring with everyone, I mean the staff people, not the cabinet, not yet?"

"Everyone wants you to stay. Desperately. They will grasp anything that might help that."

They leave it at that for the time being. No change in plans. Hernandez changes into her customary skirt suit and goes to the oval office for a meeting with some dairy industry executives. Following that she will host a delegation of Korean military leaders, confer with the Joint Chiefs of Staff, and eat lunch in-house with the chairman of the Federal Reserve. Everyone she sees will have the situation on his or her mind, but will say nothing and neither will she. It will be a long day.

2

After finally washing the night away with some scotch and soda at Ricky J's, Frank Wayne made it back to his apartment and collapsed on the couch, this time falling asleep instantly. Consequently, he was late getting to the office in the morning. Not that he had appointments or any other obligation, but regular hours was a habit and custom for him.

Kat was on the phone, but she raised her other hand in a sign of exasperation as he entered. "Yes, I will tell him as soon as he arrives," she said. Wayne waited until she hung up.

"Jesus Christ!" she exclaimed. "You will not believe what is going on. People are going nuts. I can't keep up with it."

"What are you talking about?"

"The thing you did last night," she yelled at him. "The whole world is calling you this morning about it. Most of 'em went straight to voicemail. But that must be full now." The phone rang again. Her eyes pleaded with him for help.

"Don't answer it," he said. "Is there coffee? Get us some cups and come in so we can talk about it."

"Shouldn't we clear the voicemail first?"

"We can do that with the speaker."

The voice messages varied from exaggerated praise of the video to news people feigning frenzy and requesting immediate call backs to "you won't get away with it you son of a bitch." Kat ran back to make sure the front office door was locked.

The sudden uproar was overwhelming to Wayne. Almost paralyzing. He had suddenly popped up in a place he never expected to be, playing a role that 24 hours before he could not have imagined even existed. He was not prepared to ride the wave.

But Wayne was not prone to panic. He could isolate himself mentally when it was necessary and ignore even closing in commotion that did not affect the task immediately before him. Which was Hell.

Together he and Kat determined that she should ask each caller his or her purpose and if it pertained to ASAP she would transfer the call to voice mail, making sure to clear the voice mail every fifteen minutes. When she did she was to write a quick summary of the message, which Wayne would use later to decide whether to respond. He was not going to sacrifice any of his normal professional time to ASAP. Instead he set aside one hour for it later in the afternoon.

No word from Kemal. Concerned that he might have tried to call when the line was busy and the voice mail full, and seeing no emails from him, Wayne called him. The number Kemal had given him, however, now took him straight to a voice mail message in a language he did not understand and did not recognize. His slightly educated guess was one of the many spoken in the Middle East, probably Turkish, but how should he know. It was puzzling that Kemal did not use a message that was at least partly in English, since he needed to communicate with English-speakers. Wayne left word for Kemal to call – or call again if he had already tried.

Meanwhile, he tried again to draft the complaint. The plaintiff is the proprietor of a – what to call it – business? No, the religion feature … but not itself a church. A temple? Probably not with the name Hell. Assuming they are not Satanists. If they were, they would have come up with a name more macabre than

Hell. Most likely the devil does not even call his estate Hell. Doubt if he even has a name for it. The devil is not one to refer to it objectively. He doesn't say 'Welcome to Hell'. And the devil is at home wherever he goes, so he would not be saying 'okay, guess it's time for me to get back to hell'.

Some kind of institution? Association or club? Venture or enterprise? Establishment? That might work. A religious establishment. Adequately generic. The plaintiff is the proprietor – no, the promotor, sponsor, operator … The plaintiff operates a religious establishment. He has chosen for the establishment the name Hell.

The plaintiff has invested substantial amounts of time and financial resources to establish the establishment and he is almost ready to open it to the public. However, a squad of self-righteous religion goons have taken it upon themselves to obstruct the entrance, the door, the gates of Hell. They are unlawfully occupying space directly before the entrance to the plaintiff's establishment and thereby preventing would-be patrons of Hell from enjoying the delights offered by the plaintiff. The plaintiff would describe what those delights consist of were it not for strictures of his faith that forbid him to speak publicly about what happens in Hell. Heck, even his lawyer has no idea.

Kat. Looking haggard. Handing him a stack of notes. "A friend texted me. She said there is a press rumor floating around that the president has seen the video. How about that?"

The notes recorded more of the same mixture of enthusiasm and encouragement, media requests for interviews, and "the bitch has to go – nothing pathetic losers like you can do about it." A professor of law at the University of Pennsylvania said he was very interested in the "evidence" Wayne mentioned. One person who did not leave his name identified himself as an officer in the 'American Protection Force' and warned that unless ASAP took down the video ASAP his 'unit' would 'take action' against "you and any other treasonous bastards" involved in it.

"I'm kinda scared," Kat said. "Excited. But scared."

"Talk can't hurt anybody," Wayne assured her. Still he made note to clean the Smith & Wesson .38 revolver he bought a few years ago when he first started getting work in the adult entertainment business. Other than joining him for a couple of visits to the range, the thing had rested comfortably at home in a drawer underneath other assorted items he never used any more, like his baseball glove and golf shoes. He also would need to check to see if he had any ammunition left. No permit for concealed carry, but that would not matter much if he ever had to use it.

Email from Kemal. Still working on the information. But it may be too late. Confrontation imminent.

What the heck does that mean? Wayne thought. Should he go there? What could he do? Maybe he should call the police, ask for a patrol to cruise by, defuse any trouble. No. Why should he get involved at that level? To save Jedediah's ass, as well as Kemal's?

Email from Kemal. Situation resolved for now. Friends stationed in front holding long knives. Chicken shits backed off. No Christian blood spilled … yet.

Kat. Snedicker's office called. He is going in tomorrow at 1:30 for an ex parte regarding the deposition. Put it on the calendar and remind me in the morning. Please.

Kat. Someone is knocking on the door. Ask who it is before you decide whether to open. It's a producer from some radio talk show – You're On With Angela Chellini – they want you to be a guest tomorrow afternoon at 3. In court, remember, ex parte? "But that's at –" Kat started to say, thought better of it, and sent the producer on her way with the possibility of Thursday.

More notes. More requests for interviews and/or guest

appearances. Giddy Kathy Black checking in to see if Wayne needs help. Reports the website is overwhelmed. They are working on increasing capacity. Someone from the Senate Judiciary Committee asking for his email address. No way. It might get out eventually anyway, but not if he can help it. Another threat calling Wayne's opinion "blasphemous".

When Kat went to lunch Wayne asked her to bring him a sandwich. Best if he stays in the cave today. Set the phone to route calls automatically to voice mail.

Alone, Wayne contemplated Snedicker's ex parte. Even though there had been plenty of justification for stopping the deposition – Snedicker's bad breath and vicious sneering was making Wayne's client nauseous – the judge probably would grant it and order him to produce the client again within a few days.

However, the client, who ran a small security guard company supplying "protection" for lower class strip clubs, probably would not comply and, even if he did, there was sure to be more trouble. He had confided to Wayne the last time, just before the end, that he intended to punch Snedicker in the face the next time the "asshole" got too close.

So what was the point in pursuing the matter. For that matter, Wayne mused dejectedly, what was the point of pursuing any of these matters that seemed only to delay inevitable violence of some kind. How did his practice get to that sad state? Was there not something else he could do to earn a living? Sorting mail at the Post Office. When he was a kid he went through a two-month phase dreaming of becoming a mail man. Selling cars. No, he was not good with people. Teaching. No matter what grade level the classes are full of self-entitled brats who never learned to respect anybody, much less people trying to help them learn. Besides, what subject could he teach? How to be a chump. That's what he knew best.

Like ASAP. Wayne had fallen into that one head first. He knew what he was getting into and he still let himself get suckered. Seemed amazing though that the consequences could hit so quickly. A little off the cuff speech late at night after a long day and now he apparently was a cyber star. Angela Chellini wanted him on her show – whoever she is. People wanted to attack him. The American Protection Force was coming for him. And what good will come of it? A lot of talk, a bunch of hootin' and hollerin', and that's it. The president will resign anyway, and the country will go on its wobbly way.

Kat brought him a delicious crab salad sandwich. "What's it like out there?"

"You don't want to know," she said.

More notes. Kemal saying the police are outside. Haven't done anything but talk so far. His problem with getting the information Wayne wanted was due to disagreements with his associates about what information they should provide. Maybe a meeting with everyone in Hell would help. Wednesday afternoon was the best time.

He called Kemal. Have to be in court at 1:30, but should be done by 2:30 at the latest. Meet at 3? Done. Situation? Quiet for now. Assholes are across the street. Police car parked down the block.

The Hell complaint on hold until the meeting, and expecting nothing to prevent him from writing up in the morning something responding to the ex parte, Wayne was anxious and eager to get out of the office. To the track, that's what he should do. Drive over to Laurel Park and drop a wager or two. Have a couple of beers. Relax.

"Taking off for the afternoon," he told Kat. She looked surprised.

"What about all the voice messages?" Crap! He had forgotten that horrendous growth on his life.

"Maybe tonight," he said hopefully. She was aligning her body to scold him when the phone rang. Shuffling toward the door, hoping so much to get through before it was too late. Did not make it.

"Guess who that was?" Kat announced triumphantly, stopping him abruptly. "Someone from the office of Jennifer Hernandez, Special Assistant to the President, asking you to meet with Ms. Hernandez in her office at the White House tomorrow at 2 p.m."

He felt it most acutely in his throat, immediately very dry. The crab salad processing in his stomach also grabbed his attention, burning into gas and creeping back up. The shock then jolted the back of his neck and sent a current into his brain.

The pretending terminated suddenly, as if he had crashed into a wall while sleepwalking. Play acting became real drama. The fun of contemporaneous ad lib oratory was now a frighteningly dangerous power.

Compound emotions shuddered through him: pride, excitement, fear, an almost disabling sense of inadequacy. How do I get out of this now?

"Frank?" Kat said to him concerned after he continued to stare at the floor without responding. "You okay?" He looked at her and smiled weakly.

"Yeah, I guess. Just stunned. I never expected –"

"I think it is fabulous. I am so proud." Her enthusiasm melted some anxiety.

"Thanks. But I'm not sure if – that's right, I have to be in court at 1:30 and meet with Kemal at 3. Can't do it."

"Frank, this is the president's sister. It's a matter of serious importance to the country. Of course you can do it."

He exploded, mildly, at least more than usual. Irritated at Kat, at himself, at everything. "But if I don't show up for the ex parte the judge will screw me. He'll order the deposition for

Thursday or something. And when the client finds out I didn't go he will be pissed, probably fire me. And Kemal – he's got guys with knives ready to cut people up! What the hell am I supposed to do?"

Slamming his office door behind him. Kicking the old computers and boxes of papers. Pulling the bottle of scotch from the drawer and pounding it onto his desk. Falling into his chair and staring at the bottle until the fit faded.

What choice did he have? None. He asked Kat to come in.

"I'm sorry," he said to her, noting the moisture under her eyes. "Guess even a jaded bastard like me is going to lose it once in a while."

"That's okay. I understand. What are you going to do?"

"Like you said, I have to do it. Please call the big shots back and tell them I will be there. Let me know as soon as it's confirmed, so I can get hold of Snedicker and Rafik. Just hope they appreciate my sacrifice."

But Kat put a wrench in that plan when she returned from making the call. The White House person told her that no one outside of his office and theirs must know about the meeting.

3

"Of course I remember you. You think my mind is totally defunct? Don't come all the way here just to insult me, you asshole." Marius seemed artificially stimulated when Wayne presented himself again in Room 412 of the Pennsylvania State Hospital for the Insane after an early morning drive to Norristown. On his previous visit Marius had been virtually moribund, barely able to lift his head and spending all the little energy he had just to bend forward. Now he was sitting up. And feisty.

"Jesus Christ!" he continued to rant. "Everybody assumes that the American Heretic must be utterly non compos mentis. That's bullshit.   You and your buddies in the confederate politburo can go to hell. I signed the fucking contract. The grapes are ripe. It's harvest time, senator. Let's move on."

The skin sagging off Marius' face was blanched and pasty, his pupils swollen grotesquely. What little white hair remained over his huge forehead lay flattened and greasy. The skeleton hand protruding from his gown to point at Wayne trembled and showed fingernails long and dirty and cracked. The room stunk of foul body odor and urine. The hospital staff was not taking good care of the heretic.

"Frank Wayne," Wayne finally interjected. "I was here before. Had a letter from Wilson." Marius dropped his hand and studied Wayne's face.

"From Wilson?"

"Purports to be from Wilson. I wanted you to read it – to see if you remembered writing it."

"Preposterous!" Marius shouted. "Me write you a letter? Now who's lost his mind, eh?" Then drawing back a bit and stroking his stubbly chin: "Or is this a trick? That's it! You're from the CIA. You want me to reveal the truth so a clandestine operation can take care of him. Never! Get out of here!" He fumbled with some cords attached to the bed, found a button, and pressed on it frantically.

A minute later the door opened and a giant orderly stepped in. "Escort this gentleman off the premises please," Marius howled. The orderly surveyed the situation, looked amused, and pressed Marius to lay back in the pillows.

"Why should I do that, professor?"

At once Marius' agitated demeanor switched off. Tears soaked his eyes. "I'm sorry. I'm sorry," he mumbled. Reaching out for Wayne's hand he clasped it tightly, shaking pitifully.

"I'm sorry, Mr. –" Struggling to recall the name.

"Wayne. Frank Wayne."

"Wayne. Frank Wayne. Frank Wayne." A light blinking on somewhere deep in his psyche. "Of course. Frank Wayne. Wilson wrote you a letter and you brought it here thinking that I wrote it. I remember now." And to the orderly: "Thank you so much for coming, but it's okay now. You can leave us."

"We need to get you cleaned up," the giant one said before leaving.

"To what do I owe the pleasure of this return visit? And I can assure you sir that he will be delighted to know about it."

"He? Oh you mean Wilson."

"Of course. Who else could I possibly have in mind?"

"Right." Wayne now realized that he had not planned how to approach Marius. Having decided early that morning, more or less on a whim, to come there before heading to DC for the meeting at the White House, during the drive he had contemplated only what Jennifer Hernandez might ask him, to which queries he vaguely hoped Marius could help him respond. But he had not devised any specific means of getting information from him.

"Well I want to consult with you about something."

"Consult. I like the sound of that."

Wayne then described what had happened to him over the past couple of days. As he did Marius first knotted his eyebrows and squinted at Wayne, apparently struggling to understand. Then, after Wayne had related the video episode of the night before last Marius grinned as much as his thin, cracked lips would permit and he opened his eyes wide, straining his emaciated neck muscles to nod weakly. He clasped his hands together as if about to pray.

Once Wayne said he was going to the White House for a

meeting with the president's sister Marius suddenly rose from the pillow and tried to swing his legs over the side of the bed trying to stand. Instead he tumbled from the bed onto the floor like a sack of flour. On his knees, he reached up for Wayne's hands and together they managed to erect him on his feet, the hospital gown barely hanging on to his spindly shoulders. Marius flung his arms around Wayne trying to hug him but instead latched onto Wayne's neck to keep from falling again.

At this point Wayne witnessed one of the strangest sights he had ever experienced. His attempts to describe it later quite failed to convey the extraordinary scene. Gripping Wayne's shoulders for support, Marius proceeded to dance what Wayne took to be kind of a jig. He hopped with one leg while kicking the other out to the side, then repeated the movement on each side, all the while grinning and calling out "the day .. the day .. the day is here!" This continued for about a minute, until Marius collapsed and, again with Wayne's help, fell back onto the bed.

"He will be so pleased," he muttered. "So excited. I don't know when I will see him again, but boy will he be thrilled to learn about this."

"Well, nothing's really happened yet. I don't even know specifically what she wants to talk to me about."

"Hogwash! Of course you know. She wants to know how to fix it, how to breakthrough Americans' absurd and irrational devotion to the archaic document we call a constitution and save the people's president. That's all."

It was not the time or place for it, but Wayne could not help laughing. "That's all?" he said.

"That's all," Marius repeated, apparently not affected by Wayne's reaction.

"That's fine for you to say, professor. But I'm afraid I don't know how to 'fix it' as you say."

"More baloney! You sure don't have much faith in

yourself. Where did you go to school?"

"I was in your class in law school. We talked about it the last time."

"Son, do you have any idea how many different law schools – doesn't matter. Which school?"

"Baltimore."

"Oh Jesus. Those knuckleheads have no balls whatsoever. I can't quite recall why, but they said I was loony and kicked me out on the street. Couldn't find a lawyer to take my case or I would have shut those fuckers down."

"I also finished the first year at Georgetown. After Maryland."

"Well then, you're not a total loser. Not that the Catholic fathers have less shit for brains than those Baltimore dumbasses. But you needed more discipline to make it I bet. And thank god you first learned to think like a terrapin."

His eyes gleaming, the veins down his neck swelling, his whole being practically glowing with adrenalin, Marius had metamorphosized into an animated mastermind, and he could not restrain his brilliance. But now only his lips moved.

"So here's how it happens. There does not need to be a constitutional convention in the sense of a bunch of representatives gathering somewhere to hash it all out. The whole thing can be done electronically. By the people themselves.

"You – we – somebody must draft a new version of Article II. Scrap the electoral college, the natural born citizen thing, and all the crap that has been nullified by amendment. Add a provision for recalling the president or for a no confidence vote by congress. Clarify the stuff about impeachment.

"Once there is a proposed draft it can be presented to the people, with a website that provides for comments and suggestions. The people themselves, each person individually can register her approval or rejection on specific clauses. Then there is a final vote – electronically -- on adoption or ratification, or whatever it is called. The people vote. The existing political bodies and officers are bypassed.

"Anyone can propose changes to other parts of the constitution or to add new provisions. We can incorporate the Bill of Rights into the main body. Delete the evil references and protections regarding slavery and inequality. The people can vote on a balanced budget term. The equal rights for women amendment can be incorporated in the body.

"Cannot be a liberal or conservative movement or be associated with any party or group or cause. Something for everyone. You got it?"

Wayne was not sure which Marius was talking now – the sane or the insane. So as not to commit too deeply he merely nodded ever so slightly and noted the negligible possibility of the scheme ever happening, considering the intense opposition to be expected and the eternally entrenched interests that would be sacrificed.

"Yes yes, I know. It will be like Copernicus and Galileo trying to convince the clerics and their ignorant multitudes that they are not the center of the universe. Only here the most irrational, most stubborn, most close-minded will be the so-called scholars and self-anointed experts, who will see threatened their centuries long fraudulent spin on the creation of the constitution. All those academic anemics who competed against each other to see who could eulogize the slave holders with the most fawning scholarship, who strove to surpass each previous generation in licking the balls and dicks of Madison and Jefferson. 'Heresy!' they will cry. Dost thou dare deny the divinity of these glorious deities? Question their infallibility and may they return from their golden era to strike down you miserable heretics."

Took the words right out of Wayne's mouth. What he said. Marius could see that he was getting a bit carried away. He was silent for a minute, breathing heavily.

"Sorry," he said. "It's all pent up in here, Mr. Wayne."

"Please call me Frank." Marius turned his head very slowly to look at Wayne sitting in awe beside the bed. He forced his lips into a weak smile.

"Yes, I will try to remember. Frank." Marius then launched into an extended explanation of what James Wilson did at the convention. Wilson's work is the reason the convention produced any kind of constitutional document. If he had not actually written it himself and presented it to the assemblage as a completed instrument, which the delegates could then merely tweak, the outcome of the convention would have been an amorphous mess of general propositions that could not possibly be ratified as a constitution. So that is what must happen again, Marius declared. Someone must write a new draft constitution, in plenary form. The choice given to the people must be <u>this</u> instrument, as modified through debate, or nothing.

The orderly returned and told Wayne he needed to leave for 30 minutes or so while they "cleaned up" Marius. Anticipating the traffic on I-95, Wayne said he had to leave anyway. "Cannot be late for this one," he told Marius. "But I'll be back."

"Give 'em hell Frank!"

4

Snow. Lots of it. Fat flakes falling and piling along the interstate. Driving in a muddy mist of flying sand and freezing pollutants. Maneuvering with hundreds of frantic drivers desperate to "get there" and determined not to slow down. There seemed to be an especially high voltage anxiety charging everything in motion, every driver out there pressing the horn nonstop, the baritone rattle of helicopter engines passing low overhead, traffic discipline dissolved across what used to be lanes, and urges of violence visibly emanating from tense faces.

It was a very good thing that Wayne left when he did. Barely past Wilmington traffic stopped. 10:05 a.m. Almost four hours to finish a trip that averaged about two and a half. No problem. Opportunity ... to take care of the damned ex parte and confer with Rafik. Wayne gloated over his decision yesterday to leave the problems for morning.

But no live answer at Snedicker's office. Just voicemail. Maybe this is better. "Good morning. This is Frank Wayne calling about the message we got yesterday about Mr. Snedicker going in for an ex parte appearance today at 1:30. I'm sorry, but I am out of the city all day today and cannot possibly make it for that hearing. But if Mr. Snedicker or someone else there can call me back, I'm sure we can agree on a date to continue the deposition. Look forward to hearing back from you. Thanks."

Kemal himself answered. "Frank Wayne here. Good morning." Silence. "Rafik?"

"Yes, what are you calling about, Mr. Wayne?" Terse and hostile. Not the Kemal Wayne knew. He tried to ignore the tone.

"About the meeting we have this afternoon. I am afraid I cannot—"

"There will be no meeting."

"Yeah, that's right. Something has come—"

"The meeting is canceled. We do not need you anymore."

"Oh, you mean the demonstrators are no longer demonstrating?"

"They are still here." Anger tensing his voice. "But we do not need you."

Sensing that further inquiry would be futile, Wayne nonetheless was astounded enough to press. "What is going on Rafik? Why are you firing me all of a sudden?"

Silence. Then: "You are not the person I thought. I will say no more. Good-by." Disconnected.

As he stared at the "Proud Parent of a Lincoln Middle School Honor Student" bumper sticker on the minivan that was now moving and stopping, moving and stopping ahead, Wayne mentally scanned the time since Kemal first called to spot any event that might explain this stunning development. Maybe he and his associates had concluded that they would not provide the information Wayne wanted and firing him seemed easier than any alternative. Maybe they were angry that he wanted the information in the first place. Maybe they just decided to take matters into their own hands and – but Wayne did not want to contemplate the outcome of that. Maybe it was Jedidiah.

That seemed the most likely scenario. The owners of Hell found out – probably from Jedidiah himself – that Wayne had been to see him, to try to work something out without confrontation or litigation, and they concluded from this that Wayne was more peacemaker than fighter. As proprietors of Hell naturally they wanted nothing to do with a peacemaker.

Be that as it may, at least it solved his dilemma about the meeting. But he could have used the money, that's for sure.

There was no let up of the snow. The mess became messier. Cars and trucks groped along at ten, fifteen, twenty miles an hour. Still he expected to arrive early.

Phone. Kat. Possible new client. Hallelujah. Owner of Briscoe's, which he described as a "classy" supper club near Camden Yards, served with a complaint two days ago. It alleges that the "visually-impaired" plaintiff went there for dinner with two "associates", was not allowed to enter, allegedly because he was blind, and that when he insisted two bouncers shoved him and his guests out into the street so hard that they fell into traffic, suffering serious injuries.

However, the truth, according to the owner, was that the

gentlemen were denied entrance because they were dressed like "two-bit hoods", used the work fuck in every sentence, and smelled like they had not bathed in over a month. The story about the bouncers pushing them into the street was a total lie. He was referred to Wayne by Lamont Burke.

Kat knew to ask about general liability insurance coverage. The owner, William Briscoe, "but everyone calls me 'Billy'", said that his carrier had terminated his coverage a few months ago and he had not found any since.

Kat had no word from Schnediker. She was happy to hear about Kemal.

The wind now was picking up, blowing snow off roofs and hoods and trailers, hurling it across lanes, brewing a pale and gloomy murk, slowing movement even more. A knot of anxiety began to grow in Wayne's gut. Was the trip to Norristown a mistake? He would be in DC by now if not for the diversion. He would have time to grab some lunch. As it was, he would be lucky now not to be late for the most important meeting of his life.

But that was the ridiculous feature of the drama: It was not the most important meeting of his life. It was not even important at all. The only truly noteworthy aspect of it was the glamour – of a meeting in the White House, with the president's sister, photographs of whom he had noticed, with a spark of lust, several times online.

The substance of the meeting, however, seemed to him of little significance. No extra money would be coming his way as a result of it. Nor was it likely to have even the slightest effect on the president's dilemma. She was not going to base any decision on the wacky ideas of a small-time, second-rate lawyer, especially since they were the product of a genius professor gone mad fighting to make people listen to him, and even though they originated with the man most responsible for the content of the constitution.

Then there was a matter he had not discussed with the Heretic. In the video he had shot his mouth off to say he had *evidence*. He did not have any evidence. He had a letter most certainly written by an old professor bordering on insanity in a hand imitating that of James Wilson. The knot tightened as he considered and re-considered his predicament. A fool! That's what he was.

And that's what they would call him. A fool with a lame fantasy. He was risking his life traveling through snow and ice and wind only to be on time for an event that would demonstrate to the social media millions and the multitude of American citizens duped by his oratory that he was an utter fool. Shame on you Frank Wayne. The chants echoed from the wind whipping against his windshield. Evidence? Shame on you Frank Wayne. Tear up his license. We can't have such an idiot in the Maryland Bar. He was now hoping the road would be shut down, preventing his appearance at the meeting.

Finally on the beltway at 12:50. Speed still sluggish. Mildly nauseous and hungry.

Phone. Did not recognize the number. Leave it for voicemail. "Hi Mr. Wayne. This is Rachel from Mr. Schnediker's office. He asked me to let you know that he will be appearing this afternoon for the ex parte and he will pass your message on to the judge."

What a prick. Would not even call to discuss it. Now Wayne was risking his practice as well as his life.

Baltimore-Washington Parkway 1:05. Highway 295 1:25. Sweating. Probably spots visible on shirt. Traffic still maddeningly slow. Lean on the horn bro, like everyone else. Will not part the traffic, but might help the mood.

695 1:40. Maybe, instead of trying to find parking, he could just abandon the car on the street. Mentally laughing hysterically at the idea.

395 1:45. Maine exit 1:48. Parked in garage 1:55.

Wayne ran, slid, stumbled through snow and slush and ice where the sidewalk had been cleared. Wet shoes, wet socks, wet pants. Sweaty wet shirt.

West Wing entrance 2:02. Panting like a dog. Seeing only a damp, disheveled slob, amused security blocked his steps until word came to let him through.

2:07 West Wing Lobby.

5

After leaving her sister's bedroom Tuesday morning, Jennifer Hernandez spent the rest of the day in her office: Making arrangements to ship various items back to Arizona, chatting with outside friends and colleagues about how tragic their story had become, reading and re-reading memos, articles, columns, and historical tracts concerning the incredibly frustrating lack of light on the natural born citizen clause, and monitoring the stunning proliferation of online attention ASAP and its viral video were receiving.   New electronic petitions, electronically signed apparently by hundreds of thousands, arrived in her email inbox, forwarded by other staffers, at least once every hour.   These petitions raised different related issues, but each and every one conveyed the same simple plea: Do not resign.

By early afternoon Jennifer had seen the video, or parts thereof, at least 20 times, either because she chose to or because a news clip she was watching showed an excerpt. This fueled her curiosity about Frank Wayne. So she researched what little was available through google. Maryland state bar record. Reports of a few cases he had been involved in. A newspaper article about a prominent local politician who had been arrested for soliciting prostitution in a massage parlor contained a quote from the parlor's attorney, Frank Wayne, who was described as an "adult entertainment lawyer". Not good, she thought.

Then she came across this item on a local news website:

"MAN IN VIRAL VIDEO PLEA TO PRESIDENT IS ATTORNEY FROM HELL According to a local religious leader calling himself Jedidiah, a man who made an eloquent and passionate plea for President Hernandez not to resign in a video that quickly went viral is the attorney from Hell. Jedidiah is leading a group of demonstrators who are trying to prevent some sort of club called Hell from opening. He says that Frank Wayne, whose video plea reportedly has been viewed by millions, rumored to include the president herself, is a local attorney and is representing the owners of Hell.

Jedidiah reports that his group, members of his New Life Congregation of Awakening, have met with open and virile hostility from the owners, headed by a Turkish man named Rafik Kemal. Yesterday, Jedidiah claims, Kemal sent a squad of goons with long knives out to attack the demonstrators. The police arrived in time to prevent bloodshed. Jedidiah said he has no knowledge of Wayne's role in this event. His only contact with the attorney was a short conversation Wayne initiated attempting to convince Jedidiah to call off the demonstration.

Very bad, she thought. Very bad indeed. And bizarre. And decidedly unhelpful. But she immediately was reminded of John the Baptist, who came out of the wilderness wearing only camel's hair and a leather belt and yelled at everyone like a maniac. It is the message that is important, not the messenger.

Nevertheless, she concluded, it probably would be wise to get some control over the monster before it can wreak who knows what havoc. Furthermore, she had learned well the political lesson that one should never credit without inquiry what appears in the media. Even though there was still no reason to hope that this ASAP thing would have any effect at all –the president had not even hinted at any reconsideration of her decision – it seemed wise to summon this Wayne to determine how much of a miscreant he is and, if necessary, suppress any intention he has of additional statements or acts. She instructed an assistant to set up a meeting for the following day, stressing more than once the need for secrecy.

Later in the afternoon she returned phone calls from reporters seeking inside information on the situation. Sorry, got nothing new to tell you. President's mind is made up. Friday will be moving day.

All this merely echoed what the press secretary had said repeatedly at the daily briefing. Internet videos, no matter how viral or persuasive, do not influence the president. The petitions, and other formal appeals, are to be considered more seriously, and certainly the president has or will do so, but the chances that she will change her mind because of them are negligible.

By that evening the story provided by Jedidiah had been picked up by a few other news organizations and mentioned briefly on their websites, but the facts were still largely obscure. Jennifer concluded from this that in this instance the message really was overshadowing the messenger.

Now the next morning is here and she is sitting at the breakfast table again waiting for the president to join her. She is sipping coffee and trying not to think about Frank Wayne. The president arrives, kisses her sister and adds an unusually intense hug before telling the waiter what she wants to eat. Turning again to Jennifer, she says "Well, hermana querida, pronto volveremos a ser mujeres libres."

"You mean free to clean the house and do laundry and cook?" Jennifer cannot join her sister's bittersweet mood.

"Sure. Perhaps we will be more useful that way."

Both are on the verge of crying. "Maybe we should focus on something else. By the way, let me tell you, I was very proud of myself yesterday. After our talk in the morning .. about that video thing .. I did not think about it once the rest of the day. Too busy I guess. I assume there's nothing new?"

Having considered and decided against telling her sister about the attorney from Hell, Jennifer confines her report to the online petitions pouring in. Adrianna acknowledges but says nothing about this information.

They eat breakfast in virtual silence, a sharp contrast to their customary continuous chatting. A heavy emotional vapor hovers, an aura of extreme melancholy.

"Are you going to the school with me this morning?" Adrianna says as she rises.

"Do you want me to?"

"Of course." With wet eyes Adrianna hugs her sister again and gently wipes a tear off her cheek.

The school is Marshall Elementary in Silver Spring, Maryland. The event, which commemorates Presidents' Month, has been planned since before the inauguration. The president declined to cancel it despite her impending resignation.

Snow slows the motorcade. The president is expected at 10:00 a.m. and is fifteen minutes late. But the principal is relieved when she arrives because the school district has ordered dismissal at Noon due to the weather. A couple of news vans are already parked in the lot.

She and several other teachers are waiting in a covered

area by the main entrance. Above them is a banner that reads "Welcome President Hernandez. We Love You!"

The teachers, all women, wait their turn for a handshake and a mini hug from the president and her sister. As the president reaches the last one Jennifer notices that some of the women have tears running down their faces.

The group enters the building into a long hallway, along both sides of which are lines of more teachers and other school employees. Some laugh nervously as the secret service agents scrutinize them. The president is steered down the middle of the hallway by the group, so she can only wave and smile. The few men there are somber. Jennifer again sees that most of the women are crying.

They arrive at the door to the school's gymnasium. As they enter, they hear a tremendous cheer and emerge in front of the school's 800 students assembled on bleachers and the floor. Above them is another, larger banner with the same message.

The students are clapping and cheering, and some are chanting "We love you President Hernandez." Scattered among the students are hand-drawn signs that individual students are raising periodically. The signs read "Please Do Not Resign!" Jennifer is very moved and notes that her sister is too.

After about five minutes the principal steps to a microphone and holds her hands in the air signaling for quiet. The students settle down enough for her to speak.

"Boys and girls, I can see that you know how special this day is for us. I don't think Marshall Elementary has ever had a day like this. It's so wonderful for you to let our guest know how excited we are to have her here today. But you need to remember our instruction. Very important. Please do not display any signs that may be seen as political." She turns to the president and winks. The president and her sister laugh. "So it is my incredible honor to introduce the first woman and the first Hispanic -- and the first mom -- President of the United States."

The rowdy applause and cheering begin anew, as does the raising of signs, notwithstanding the principal's admonition.

After thanking the principal and introducing her sister, the president talks to the students about what a president is and does and how one is chosen, about how the founders got together and came up with a miraculous constitution in only three months, and about the important place of presidents Washington and Lincoln in the history of the country. Then she concludes by explaining how a person is honored and privileged to become president, that the president must obey the law just like everyone else, and that no president has the right to be president. Much of what she says goes over many of the kids' heads, but the television news crews lurking about the sides of the gym demonstrate that they are not her only audience.

As originally planned, the president was to take three questions from the students following her talk. She had since decided against this part of her visit, so now she moves away from the microphone to leave the gym. The principal, however, knowing nothing of this change of plans, tells the three students who had been designated to ask the questions to stand and, respectfully, state the questions. The president, somewhat embarrassed, returns to the microphone.

The first student, a boy of about ten, tells the president that he would like to be president someday, and asks what qualities he will need to develop. The president responds by emphasizing the importance of good learning habits, most importantly in school, but also in life generally. She then condenses all that she meant to say into: "But I believe that to be president, and to be successful at anything in life, there are two primary requirements: You must believe in yourself and you must have courage."

The next student, a girl of about the same age, looks puzzled. She glances at the principal, assumes a determined expression, and, with a distraught tone, blurts out "Is that why you're quitting? Because you don't believe in yourself and don't have courage?"

A collective gasp fills the gym, followed by anguished murmurs, some angry. Reaction by the principal is immediate. Her face colors as she steps past the president to the microphone. The student is crying even before she hears the principal say harshly "No Katrina. That is not acceptable, and you know it. Report to my office now!"

Jennifer can see that her sister is stunned, frozen in place, unable to discern exactly what is happening. She grabs her sister's hand and leads her away from the scene. The principal catches up to them and says "I am so sorry."

Recovering her presence of mind, the president tells the principal not to apologize and not to punish the girl. After all, she had the temerity to say what everyone probably is thinking. Pretty gutsy for a young girl.

The principal now is emboldened to explain. "Perhaps we should have canceled. You see, we are having great difficulty making the students understand what is happening. They all love you. Especially the girls. Their teachers have talked and talked to them about how all of us, even you, must follow the constitution. But they don't buy it. The bright ones like Katrina keep saying why, if it doesn't make sense."

The president thanks the principal for speaking so frankly and continues on her way to the limo, surrounded by women smiling and weeping at the same time.

Neither sister talks during the drive back to the White House. When they arrive the president goes to her private rooms without saying a word to anyone.

Jennifer returns to her office in the West Wing. It is 12:30. She has a number of minor matters to take care of before meeting with Frank Wayne at 2:00.

A quick scan of news websites and her email inbox shows that the crescendo of popular pleading for the president to stay in office has not diminished. Much of it refers to ASAP and the Wayne video. Some of it asserts different arguments.

Since she last checked the inbox, about three hours ago, almost 200 new messages have appeared, the vast majority of which are from people wanting information, like reporters, news producers, members of congress, or groups of people vehemently declaring, via petitions or joint letters, their desire that the president not resign. She has no time right now to respond, so puts it off for later in the afternoon, although she does not know if she will have time then either.

It is now 1:30. She asks an assistant to bring her a sandwich and she eats it while watching the Wayne video again. Expecting Wayne to be brash and ill-mannered, she is not looking forward to his arrival.   In the video he appears too self-confident, presumptuous, even arrogant. This will not be an easy meeting. Maybe he will be early, so she can get it over with quicker. But this is unlikely if he is coming from Baltimore, in the snow.

Jennifer is not even clear on what she hopes to accomplish. She does not anticipate additional enlightenment on the resignation issue from an adult entertainment attorney from Hell. Perhaps if he will just agree not to make any more videos and to let the matter alone.

One bit of information she definitely wants to get from Wayne is what the evidence is that he claimed in the video to have regarding the expectations of the framers.   She is extremely skeptical about this. More than 200 years of work by scholars and others surely has uncovered every scrap there could be of such evidence.   And the president's dream team of lawyers that supposedly has researched the matter exhaustively again came up with nothing new. Yet this hack strip club attorney claims to have something no one else has found. Absurd.

1:50. Jennifer tells the West Wing receptionist to let her know if Wayne arrives early. She has become strangely nervous and expectant.

2:00. No Wayne yet. He is late.

2:05. She checks with the receptionist -- because she hates waiting. Now a little angry.

2:07. Receptionist announces that he is here.

However, when Jennifer tells the receptionist to bring Wayne into her office the receptionist warns that he is very wet and messy. Says he ran through snow and slush.

Her door is open. So as the receptionist says "here is Mr. Wayne" she looks up and there is Frank Wayne. Wearing a well-used dark blue wool suit damp and darker in splotches and a solid red tie with blue dots. His cheeks and forehead are pink from the cold. Unkempt dark brown hair touching his ears and falling across his forehead until he brushes it back with his fingers. Chin not shaved, showing rough stubble. Still out of breath, he seems visibly embarrassed.

"How do you do, Mr. Wayne. Thank you for coming." She shakes his hand, winces at the cold touch, and adds: "Don't you use gloves?"

"Yes, sometimes," he says, "not today. Wasn't expecting this weather. The pleasure is mine, Ms. Hernandez."

"Or a coat?" Jennifer feels surprising empathy for Wayne and views his state as somewhat comical.

Shrugging sheepishly, he says "Didn't plan well. It's been a crazy week."

"That may be a bit of an understatement. Please sit down." Wayne looks uncertainly at the chair she points to, obviously reluctant to plant his wet suit in it. "Don't worry about that, Mr. Wayne. The chair will be someone else's problem in a few days."

"So it's really going to happen?" He seems genuinely

unhappy.   She puts on the best droll, ironic façade she can manage.

"I am afraid so. My sister has decided, and it appears that her mind is locked shut to any objections. Yours included, despite the phenomenal response it has provoked."

"Yeah, another thing I didn't plan on. If anyone had told me this would happen, I would never have agreed to do it. Politics and all that is not my thing. I should a just hid out at the club like I had in mind."

"The club?"

"Oh, just a club I sometimes hang out at, have a couple of drinks. They know me. Wouldn't give me up." Jennifer is acutely puzzled. What the heck is this guy talking about?

"I'm afraid I don't quite understand. Why would you want to hide out?"

"Because they wanted me to do that video and I was trying to avoid having to do it. You see, Ms. Hernandez, I am not a political guy. I was just minding my own legal business on Monday, not a thought about all this. And this guy I know, former client, starts arguing with me, like he always does, we were at a lunch place, and all of a sudden I'm blabbering all this stuff like I said in the video. Well, later some lady calls me and asks me to come to a meeting. I would never have done it, but my secretary convinced me just to go and see what's up. So I went and got roped into giving another speech, if you want to call it that. I still tried to get out of it and was leaving for Ricky J's – that's the club – but my secretary showed up at my place and, well, I ended up doing it. Don't know how. I didn't have anything prepared. Just did it spontaneously." He pauses. "Sorry. I gave you more explanation than you wanted."

Astonished by Wayne's tale, Jennifer suspects it is not true. But the more she stares incredulously at him, with a pointed expression of skepticism, she sees a phlegmatic and utilitarian man, driven by the need to get things done rather than make things up. Lacking discipline to be sure. However, not a man of fancy. A genuine straight talker.

"That is an incredible story, Mr. Wayne. I assumed – I'm sure most people who saw it assumed – that it was a well-planned production." He is touched by the comment and smiles timidly.

"No. Maybe that's why it worked. I don't know. But one more thing … I was reluctant to do it, but I spoke from the heart. I believe deeply everything I said." Now Jennifer is touched. She senses some emotion rising and stifles it. "And I believe I also spoke from authority."

"Yes, that's one matter I wanted to talk about. You said you had evidence. Tell me about that."

Wayne rubs his eyes and takes a deep breath, then gazes into Jennifer's eyes like he is testing her sincerity, whether he can trust her. Clearly he prefers not to discuss the subject.

"That's what you had me come for?"

"No. Not that only. I had in mind to dissuade you from doing anything more to promote your ideas. But it sounds like you are not likely to do anything further. Since you regret what you already have done." This remark upsets Wayne.

"I didn't say I regretted it. I don't. I just wouldn't have done it if I had seen into the future and what would happen. Like I said, I strongly believe in what I said. President Hernandez should not resign. It will be an unnecessary tragedy … for the country … and her … and you for that matter."

Again Jennifer is affected and has to dismiss an urge to hug Wayne. "On behalf of my sister, and myself, I appreciate those sentiments. And I thank you for your part in showing us how they are shared by so many. But you see, the president feels that she has no choice. The constitution says what it says, and she swore to uphold it. No one has offered any real ground she can believe in to take such an extraordinary, unprecedented, and perhaps dangerous leap."

Wayne suddenly seems more alert.   He sheds his despondency and a flash of inspiration sparks a gleam in his eyes. "Please do not take this as disrespectful, but how much do you and your sister know about how the constitution was created? I mean in detail. Who did what at the convention. That sort of thing."

Jennifer does feel a bit disrespected, but does not show it. "Well I guess you can't say either of us is a constitutional history scholar, but I know she has studied it over her career. And, as you know, she has had a panel of the most distinguished constitutional lawyers and scholars working overtime on this. So—"

"Do you know what James Wilson did at the convention?"

She senses a trap, but it is not avoidable. "Who?"

Wayne eases back in the chair with a satisfied smile. "James Wilson wrote the constitution, almost single-handedly."

"What are you talking about?" She does not like being at a disadvantage with this relatively insignificant person and is impatient for him to make his point.

"The convention delegates came up with a few general resolutions then assigned a Committee of Detail to write up a draft constitution with them. Gave them about a week to do it and adjourned. As usual with committees, most of the members made suggestions, but only one did the work. It came down to the Saturday before the Monday the convention expected the draft. On that Saturday Wilson wrote the constitution, by himself. It was printed the next day and passed out on Monday."

"That is a preposterous story." Now she is very irritated and feels that he is trying to beguile her. But he suggests that she go to a website at treasures.constitutioncenter.org and click on *Manuscript of the Committee of Detail Report, August 3, 1787.*

"You will see there the very document – in Wilson's

handwriting -- and the explanation that he wrote it. I am not making this up, madam." He waits while she looks. The website is maintained by the National Constitution Center in Philadelphia. Displayed are documents from the Historical Society of Pennsylvania. They include the one Wayne mentioned, with a link that she uses to bring up the pages of the draft constitution as written by James Wilson.

No longer suspicious of Wayne's motives or intentions, actually fascinated by what she is seeing, and highly puzzled at why she does not recognize the name of this obviously instrumental founder, Jennifer nevertheless cannot see how this affects her sister's predicament. No doubt people more learned in the area than she, notably the distinguished panel of experts that has been working on the issue, know all about this Wilson and what he did and do not find any relevance for it.

"Ok. I see it. And I admit, frankly, to ignorance on my part about this. Be that as it may, however, I fail to discern the relevance of this information to the situation facing my sister."

"Let me explain. First, there is the fact that most of the constitution was composed in one day by one man. Doesn't that say something about whether its authors intended that each word, no matter how unreasonable it might eventually be, should be obeyed literally forever and ever? And can anyone legitimately believe that this man understood that he was writing in stone, decreeing discreet rules every succeeding generation must follow regardless of the future circumstances? The absurdity speaks for itself." Jennifer was rivetted.

"Second, and this is where the evidence comes in. I have a letter that appears to be in Wilson's handwriting. It is dated around the time of his death. The letter declares Wilson's anxiety over this very matter. It clearly demonstrates that he would find inconceivable this blind adherence to the constitution as a sacred instrument.

"He wants the people to be able to deem nullified provisions that clearly are senseless or to change the wording without the impossible process for a formal amendment. He envisions new versions of the constitution as development of the nation warrants. This bears directly on the president's response to the news about her birth. The people adore your sister. They want her to be their president. She must hang on and fight to retain the office.

"This might lead to further revisions or even a new convention. It can be a virtual convention, with the people logging in to comment and vote on proposed provisions. There are so many possibilities now. How can this great electronic age still be ruled by an archaic set of rules gathered together by a group of old white men living in essentially pre-historic times?"

He stops. Finally. Apparently realizing how he had again launched a long-winded rant, he is visibly embarrassed. Putting his hands over his face, he says "I am so sorry. I should not have gone on like that. I don't know what brought that on. Maybe I better go." He stands up.

Momentarily stunned by the force of Wayne's monologue, Jennifer experiences a medley of reactions, to what he said and to him. She marvels at the irony of what she had expected before meeting him. He is not the boorish jester she anticipated. Indeed, he is serious and thoughtful.

The substance of his argument seems artful, too good to be true, like a very well-constructed fantasy, the product of a modern-day Don Quixote musing about constitutional processes he knows nothing about. She should thank him for his suggestions and send him on his way. And, as if reading her mind, he is standing before her about to leave.

But some element of his presentation registers true. She is not sure what. So she does not want the meeting to end just yet.

"Tell me something, Mr. Wayne. Are you really the

attorney from Hell?" This startles him, thrusts him even more on the defensive.

"Not anymore. Client fired me today. How did you know about that?" She laughs at his naivete.

"They have this thing now. It's called the internet. Drop the name Frank Wayne into google and voila. Short news article about your video and someone named .. Jedidiah, if I remember correctly. He called you the attorney from Hell."

"Yet more publicity I don't need." Wayne seems depressed now, anxious to leave. But Jennifer is still not quite done with him.

"This letter you mentioned. Do you have it with you now?"

"No. It's in a safe place."

"How did you acquire it?"

"Just came in the mail." She does not believe him and tilts her head as if to say do not mock me. "That's what happened, madam. Not making it up. You can ask my secretary."

She studies Wayne as he shuffles wearily towards the door. There is still something that is not settled. Should she tell her sister about him? Might she want to hear him? Highly doubtful. But the weather will make his return an ordeal.

"Mr. Wayne," she calls to him before he is gone. "Would it be possible for you to stay in Washington tonight? If we get a room for you?" Because Adrianna being interested is such a remote possibility, she does not want to mention it to him. "Traveling back tomorrow will be much easier."

He thinks it over. "Yes, that would be nice. Thank you. It has been an exhausting day."

It has been a long night for the president. Three hours sleep at most, scattered in segments measured in minutes. She tried to work on the speech promised for the next evening, but struggled futilely to concentrate. Waking dreams of so many scenes from her life played like a fractured documentary in her mind, some amusing, some terribly sad. Several times she slept only to wake up crying and having no idea why.

She considered asking Jennifer to come, but could not because she did not want to burden her sister more than she already had.

She did not re-open the mental debate over the decision. Indeed, since she returned to the White House from the school visit she has adamantly refused even to think about it. Only the content of the speech troubled her, not the substance of the announcement. She was firm, decided, resolute.

At least consciously.

Now she is once again sitting with her sister in front of breakfast, although neither has touched the food. They have exchanged only routine desultory chit chat. The atmosphere is at once tense, somber, and excruciatingly depressed.

Adrianna urges Jennifer to eat. Jennifer returns the plea. She wants to mention her talk with Frank Wayne, but is afraid to trip any emotional wires her sister has strung about her. However, she can see that Adrianna is not well. Her eyes are puffy and red. Every movement she makes, with her hands, her shoulders, her head, is quick and jerky, a sure sign of overwrought nerves and, could it be? – fear. Now worried about the president's health, physical and mental, Jennifer decides to engage her in hopes of drawing out some of the anxiety.

"I met with Frank Wayne yesterday."

At first it appears that Adrianna did not hear. Then she tilts her head smugly and speaks with uncharacteristic sarcasm. "And who is that, John's great grandson? No, maybe it's Bruce

Wayne's. Don't tell me Batman is coming to the rescue."

Jennifer is quite irked by this response. But she clings to the moment and proceeds. "Ha ha. He is the guy that did the video. You know, the message to you that went so viral."

Now Adrianna is laughing viciously – at Jennifer. "You've got to be kidding, little sister. It's a joke, right?"

Jennifer tightening, her face coloring. Rarely angry, but here it is. "What do you mean, a joke? Is there something funny about it?"

"Come on, mujer. You met with some guy who thinks he has the answers and you expect me to take you seriously." Eyes wide and shining. Brows knotting together. Pressured fury, set to detonate.

"My god, Adrianna. You're talking to me like—"

"Like you're being incredibly stupid. It all seems so simple to you. All I have to do is refuse to leave and everything will be honey and flowers. We'll all sing happy hymns and dance around the Rose Garden. Unbelievable." Now shaking her head in disgust.

Jennifer breathless, eyes wet, feeling deep hurt, nothing ever before suffered from her sister. She wants to escape the scene. To get out. To run for her office, where she can cry, unrestrained by the red-faced monster staring at her and trembling. A voice straining to be heard through the anguish squeezing her mind, telling her this is not her sister Adrianna. It is a demon that has seized her soul.

Jennifer slowly stands and backs away in fear. The president remains seated, still glaring icy hot.

"Madam President," Jennifer stammers acidly. "You do whatever the hell you want. Don't look for help from me anymore. Go on back to Arizona. Maybe you can become president of the PTA. Or not. Maybe no one will want to help you there either. You won't even listen to Frank Wayne, or anyone else for that matter. You won't even consider anything but running away. Until this moment I believed you were the bravest woman ever. Now it seems like you're just a scared little girl. Good luck."

About to slam the door behind her. Adrianna screams: "That's right! I will do whatever the fuck I want! If Jordan wants this fucking job so much he can fucking have it!"

Back in her office Jennifer collapses on the couch and cries passionately, bitterness stinging her tears.

Back in her bedroom Adrianna collapses on the bed and cries, her conscious mind in frightening chaos. She has canceled every activity planned for that day and shudders for the gloomy hours still to come. At least the intense weeping drains her agitation. She falls asleep.

And dreams. She is in the presidential limousine, moving through a raucous crowd of demonstrators who are shouting horrible things at her, but while she feels the anger, she cannot hear the words. A call comes in from a Homeland Security agent telling her they have Jennifer in custody and that agents have staked out her parents' home, pending her order to proceed with the arrests. The children and her husband will be rounded up before dusk. She tries to say that it is all a big mistake, but instead she congratulates the agent and expresses satisfaction that the plan is coming to fruition.

Now the motorcade accelerates, although still amidst the people, who shriek and attempt to jump out of the way, but many are mowed down, some probably dead. The escort turns a corner. However, the limousine continues alone. Through violent gusts of wind that whip hail against the windows. The vehicle is moving faster and faster, scaring Adrianna and making her curl up with her head buried between her knees. She wants to shout for help, but gags and begins to shake. The limousine will crash. There is no doubt.

Then suddenly it stops, abruptly, no braking or skidding. When she looks she is back in the oval office sitting at the desk, still shaking. Jennifer is standing before her with two men, one tall and muscular wearing a plain dark blue suit, the other a grizzled and creepy old man in an outfit that could have been imported from the 18th Century, complete with a dirty wig and scratched up wire spectacles.

"Madam President," Jennifer says sarcastically. "This is Frank Wayne and James Wilson. You would not see them, so I brought them here to spite you, bitch."

"Madam President," the old man says. "I beg you to excuse my appearance. You see, I have not eaten or changed clothes or bathed for 230 years, and I know it shows. However, I pray that my offensive physical figure will not diminish the message I bring to you. Which is that you must not leave this lovely office. If all of my colleagues could have come here with me I am sure they would all think it an immense tragedy if you resign because of a trivial statement that we added, without consideration, to the constitution towards the end of an unbearably hot summer and the conclusion of a project we just wanted to get done. We did not write eternal commandments. None of us believed that we were wiser than our descendants would be. None of us, I especially, had even a fraction of the knowledge and wisdom the people have now. Don't let ancient ghosts like me determine the future of this country. I plead for you to answer the call of the people. To continue as their president."

With that speech the ghost fades away.

"Adrianna," Frank Wayne has the nerve to address her. "You are so much more beautiful in person. I hope that you will stay in Washington so we can get together soon some evening."

Just then a door blasts open and Mike Jordan steps in armed with an assault rifle and ordering everyone out. But Frank

Wayne punches him in the stomach and hits him in the chin with a powerful uppercut.   Jordan staggers backwards before regaining position and charging back at Wayne. Adrianna begins to shout "Stop! Stop!" and wakes up.

When Jennifer calms down, she is left feeling empty. She is not motivated to do anything. Does not care what happens to the Hernandez presidency. Begins to imagine a different life. Working on someone's campaign for Arizona state treasurer. Or director of the Oro Valley Arizona Chamber of Commerce. Maybe she can write a memoir: The inside story of the only administration shorter than that of William Henry Harrison.

Asking her assistant to let Frank Wayne know he will not be needed today and that he can go home to crawl under the rock he came out from, buzzing back to make sure she left the last part out, to which her assistant responded with "Duh", Jennifer gradually realizes that she is not bitter about her sister's treatment. Instead she feels deep sympathy and a powerful desire to help ease Adrianna's pain.   But she knows that, unless requested, there is nothing further she can do in the circumstances.

Her assistant: Frank Wayne is on the phone asking if she wants a copy of the document they talked about yesterday. When he gets to his office he can have his secretary scan and email it. Ok. Thank him and tell him I appreciate all his trouble.

She returns to a list she started the day before of items to complete before the move out.

Just before Noon the West Wing receptionist informs her that something has arrived for her and asks if the delivery person can bring it to her office. As long as it's not ticking, she says. There is a knock. Come in. She cannot see the person through all the roses he carries – red, yellow, pink – must be three dozen reaching out from two silver and turquoise vases. They are stunning and most fragrant. She opens the card. "Lo siento

mucho mi querida hermana. Te amo. Por favor perdoname.
Adrianna. PS. Please be there tonight."

A short time later the email from Wayne arrives with a
copy of the letter attached. She forwards it to her sister without
reading the letter and with only this explanation: "Letter Frank
Wayne received purporting to be written by James Wilson. PS.
Thank you so much for the beautiful roses. I love you too. I will
be there."

Meanwhile, Wayne has made it to his office, where Kat
shows him a notice of ruling that was delivered by messenger
earlier in the morning. The notice states that the judge granted
Snedicker's unopposed ex parte application to compel Wayne to
produce his client for further deposition and that the deposition
must occur within seven days. The judge also issued an order to
show cause why Wayne should not be sanctioned in the amount
of $2,000 for terminating the deposition without cause and
ignoring Snedicker's efforts to reschedule it.

"This really sucks," he says and asks Kat to contact the
client about which day will be best for him.

"How did your meeting at the White House go?"

"Scintillating," he responded with a smirk. "But pointless
and fruitless."

"You mean she's going to resign?"

"Yep. Looks that way. Whatever. My part in this drama
is done. Now I need to make some money."

He returns the call from Billy, owner of Briscoe's. They set
up a meeting for the following afternoon.

He writes up a nasty letter to Snedicker, accusing him of
deceit and lack of civility and advising that he too would resort to
an ex parte appearance in order to acquaint the judge with all the
lies. Then he has a long phone conversation with the client, who
confirmed a date with Kat, but wanted to talk to Wayne. Wayne
tries to explain what happened. The client does not care. He is

not mad at Wayne, but warns that he likely will "beat the crap out" of Snedicker if his behavior does not change.

By 3:30 he has had enough office time. He goes home, stopping to pick up some Chinese food on the way, which he eats while watching the early news, which is all about the president's resignation speech coming up at 9. The only live sports he can find is the University of Maryland Terrapins women's team against Penn State, but the Terps are blowing out the Lions by 30 points. So once he is full of Chinese food he takes a nap. When he wakes after an hour he cannot think of anything else to do, so he changes clothes and goes to Ricky J's.

There he is a celebrity because of the viral video. Several regulars accost him and try to shake his hand or slap him on the back. But he wants nothing to do with that now and lets them know it. Everyone backs off, he takes a seat at the bar, and orders a scotch and soda.

There is a television over the bar tuned to some news channel. Wayne sees video of large crowds and is close enough to hear the broadcast:

"There is quite the phenomena taking shape across the country this afternoon and evening. From Washington, D.C. to Chicago to San Francisco tens of thousands, maybe hundreds of thousands, of demonstrators have taken over the streets expressing their disapproval of President Hernandez' decision to resign from office in the wake of revelations about the country of her birth. Our first report is from Paula Cornel in Washington.

"The scene here is electric, Dick. We have crowd estimates of more than 500,000 people jamming 16th Street from Lafayette Square to the National Mall. So far it's a peaceful demonstration, marked by an unprecedented diversity of participants: Young professionals in suits to blue collar workers in overalls to seniors, some pushing walkers. I asked a few why they are here. The answers were consistent and emphatic: To let the president know how profoundly disappointed they are. Melanie Jenkins is in Chicago.

"A similar scene here, Paula. Only I have heard estimates of more than 700,000 people packing Michigan Avenue. So far noisy but peaceful here too. No leaders. No loudspeakers. No oratory. Just a spontaneous mass outpouring of emotion. I have seen many people in tears. Now to Drew Canby in San Francisco.

"Melanie, I am standing on a stone wall in front of the federal building here and there are people crowded across Golden Gate Avenue, Polk Street, and filling the plaza in front of City Hall. I have covered many demonstrations here, but I have never seen the likes of this. Here too no one in charge, no organizers. A massive assembly of people. Not angry. Only very very sad. Many crying and hugging each other. The ones I spoke too responded quite like those Paula mentioned: How can this be happening, they say. Back to you Dick.

"Thank you Drew, Melanie, and Paula. We should note that similar events are occurring in many other cities, with reports coming in of almost one million people in some places. Truly an unprecedented expression by the American people. Apparently, it will have no effect, however, as we have received no information from the White House indicating any change in the president's intention to resign. Here is our chief White House correspondent, Simone Guiterrez. What do you have for us, Simone?

"Well Dick, only this: I have been told that congressional leaders of both parties will be here shortly for a brief meeting with the president. No word on what is to be discussed. But presumably it will be some sort of formal notification of the resignation before it is announced to the public by her speech coming up in about 90 minutes. I will let you know if I hear anything more definite.

"Simone, has there been any word at all about the

administration's response to these incredible demonstrations? Have you been told whether the president is aware of them or is watching?

"None whatsoever, Dick. The president remains tightly secluded. I am not sure that even her closest advisors are communicating with her right now. It appears that she has made up her mind and does not want anyone suggesting second thoughts at the last minute."

Jennifer Hernandez has spent the past few hours struggling to keep occupied with a variety of mundane matters. The surreal hours have dragged. She has not communicated further with her sister. She learned about an hour ago that some congressional leaders had met with her for 15 minutes then left without saying a word to anyone, despite the mob of reporters closing on them with barrages of questions.

Now she is sitting in an anteroom to the Oval Office, waiting for the president to appear. There are only three other people there, all very long-time aides who have known each other well for years. Yet none of them speak. And there is no other sound – until a door opens and the president enters.

She is wearing a dark red wrap dress with a v-neckline and short sleeves, a simple but elegant necklace of silver and turquoise, her dark hair newly done with graceful curls reaching just below her shoulders, her face and eyes radiant and bright. She goes directly to Jennifer, smiles coyly, hugs her, and, holding her sister's hand, says "How do I look?"

"Brilliant and ravishing." Adrianna chuckles.

"Watch this," she says, pointing towards the Oval Office. Motioning for Jennifer to follow, she proceeds into the room where several people are twiddling with broadcast equipment. "Are we ready?" she says to them.

"We are ready when you are, Madam President. It is 8:55." Adrianna takes her place behind the presidential desk. She has no papers.   This talk will be from memory or spontaneous. Jennifer stands behind the lights.

Four scotch and soda refills have floated Frank Wayne's consciousness. He feels detached from the reality closing on him in the form of bodies huddling into reach of the television audio. Glancing at the screen he is aware that the president is about to speak, but he wants neither to watch nor hear. He avoids watching by stumbling from the bar into a chair facing away from the television. But he cannot avoid hearing as the bartender turns up the volume.

"Good people of this magnificent country. Thank you so much for listening to what I have to say to you tonight. I am announcing a decision I have made about whether to continue serving as your president in light of the discovery, as startling to me as it was to you, that I was born in Mexico and brought into Arizona a few days later.

"This decision has been by far the most difficult I have ever had to make. I have received excellent opinions from many experts and non-experts, many influential political leaders, and vast numbers of ordinary citizens. While these opinions have varied widely, and offered incisive points on all sides of the issue, I am grateful that so many thousands of you, if not millions, have urged me to stay in office.

"I have in particular wished to consult with persons whose knowledge of the creation of our constitution might provide some sense, some meaning, for the so-called natural born citizen clause that compels me to make this decision. As you know, that clause states that 'no person except a natural born citizen shall be eligible to the office of president'.

"I called on a team of the most distinguished lawyers and legal scholars we have to determine if these words could be interpreted in a manner that would make them inapplicable to my circumstances. These experts concluded that the clause cannot be so interpreted. The statement means exactly what it says.

"I also called on this team, as well as many other scholars and historians, to scrutinize the history of the constitution for any evidence or precedential opinion that might support a contention that the authors of the constitution did not intend the clause to apply in circumstances like mine, notwithstanding the plain meaning of the language they used. No such evidence or opinion has been presented to me.

"Consequently, it appears that under the natural born citizen clause of our constitution I am not eligible to hold this office and I must resign. As a loyal citizen of this country, which I love with all my heart, I am bound to obey its constitution. Indeed I swore to preserve, protect, and defend it.

"Nevertheless, I cannot act without acknowledging another view that has come to my attention only in the past few days. The proponents of this view have caused me to realize how little we really know about the thoughts of those who spent the summer of 1787 drafting the constitution. Our sole source of information about these proceedings are notes prepared by James Madison and published only decades later.

"Madison has been proclaimed over the generations as the father and principal author of the constitution. I have learned, however, that Madison was not the principal author. I have learned that another man was. His name was James Wilson. It is not a familiar name. Since he died alone and on the run from debt collectors, Wilson has been utterly blotted out of memory by historians, scholars, and politicians.

"Another fact that surely explains the repression of Wilson's contribution in favor of Madison's is that Wilson vehemently opposed slavery and any expression of support for it in the constitution. Madison, on the other hand, owned more than 100 slaves and made sure that the constitution protected the slave trade.

"I am convinced that if we could divine the mind of Wilson, and perhaps other delegates like him, we would learn that they never intended their work that summer to be the final word, that they did not believe they were creating eternal commandments, and most significantly, that they did not assume to know more about good government than their descendants would after decades of practice and experience. They created a constitution to get the country up and running, not to bind future generations of Americans to every word they hastily included to get the document finished.

"I believe that if Wilson and the others were here right now they would tell me that resigning as president because of the natural born citizen clause would be an absurd and tragic act. They would declare that if such a result is mandated by the constitution then the constitution is flat wrong and should be disregarded.

"I cannot disregard a constitution that I am sworn to protect. But I also cannot disregard the will of the very people who ordained and established that constitution in the first place. The fundamental principle upon which this nation was founded was articulated anew by our greatest president amidst the consuming fire that marked its rebirth: This is a government of the people, by the people, and for the people.

"The people themselves are the ultimate sovereign. The constitution is merely an expression of their will. The people can, and should, revise or remake it as they believe to be appropriate. I believe that the time has finally come for the people to express their will again, in a new constitution, substantially identical to the existing one, but purged of all elements that no longer belong and featuring those new elements the people deem necessary to governing this great country in the 21st Century and beyond.

"Therefore, I come to the announcements I promised you. First, I will not resign this office unless and until it is proven to me that existing authority, constitutional or otherwise, obligates me to do so or that the people desire that I do so.

"Second, I will use my executive power to appoint a purely bipartisan commission and delegate it to draft a proposed new constitution, which will then be presented to the people for their approval, rejection, and proposals for changes. This process will be in effect a new constitutional convention, except that this time all the people will participate -- through electronic communications that were not even imagined by the original delegates as they made their arduous journey to Philadelphia.

"The commission will be a new Committee of Detail, modeled after the original that resulted in a draft constitution written by James Wilson and presented to the 1787 convention delegates for their consideration. Further information and the names of those to be appointed will be forthcoming from my office in the coming days.

"Naturally I do not expect my decisions to be unanimously approved. There surely will be many objections, and probably legal proceedings to challenge them, as is rightful in a great democracy like ours. I only pray that the debate remains considerate and peaceful and that it reflects the best of who we proud Americans are.

"Thank you for listening and may God bless the United States of America."

www.ingramcontent.com/pod-product-compliance
Lightning Source LLC
Chambersburg PA
CBHW060439180626
46817CB00007B/2901